I0656512

TABLE OF CONTENTS

PROJECT BLIGHT: COLLAPSE

ARIZONA TO TEXAS

SAKAI GIVENS

ACKNOWLEDGMENTS

Special thanks to illustrator Eva Jongepier for bringing my vision of my characters to life. Your talent and creativity have added a whole new dimension to my project, and I'm truly grateful for your amazing work!

CAST

APOLLO VICE

AKIRA YAMI

ISIS SAFIYA

VI

ENA HIDEYO

AKIM VOK

DIANA SLAVIK

TOMIE SHIMA

XIV

SETH RA

XV

XVI

BLIGHT

Texola, Oklahoma

They made it to the entrance of Texola, Oklahoma which seemed like a ghost town, and got out of the vehicles to look for somewhere to bunker for the night. They were exhausted, hungry, and sleep deprived. Why was the military so afraid to enter Oklahoma? Seth had a bad feeling in his gut. Something didn't feel right... something was off. Seth looked over at the group, as something charged full speed at Apollo. They slid to the floor. Everyone stood there as something... no someone hovered over Apollo. Seth and the others were heavily fatigued and struggled to activate their *blight*. The creature stood over Apollo as the moonlight shone on its' face.

It spoke in a withered voice, and uttered the words, "I found you."

The team could see that although the creature resembled a person it was not. The nails and teeth were as sharp as knives, the clothes were stained with dry blood. It appeared to be some type of animal, human hybrid and when it spoke those three words, the voice was oddly familiar.

The thing that shook them to their core was his eyes, he had the *blight*. The membrane that covered the creatures' eyes were black, and his iris was purple and dim. They bore into one's soul in a way that appeared aggressive. As Apollo tried to crawl away, Seth asked, "What are you?"

The question seemed to irritate the creature, and it mumbled, "after everything you really don't remember me? YOU ALL THOUGHT I WAS WEAK!" The creature paced back and forth near Apollo's body. "I just wanted to be as strong as all of you, I just wanted to be capable of protecting my friends, just like you Seth."

As the creature finished his sentence Seth put the pieces together and remembered. Seth then said softly, "Brian?"

Meanwhile, a few months ago at Hex University, New Jersey

Tomie Shima, an Asian African American woman stood at 5'10, was athletically toned, with curly black hair that reached halfway down her back. She had skin the color of bronze, and eyes that shone a hazel green color. Apollo Vice, a 5'10 Caucasian man with gray eyes, short, straight brown hair, was wearing sweatpants and a white t-shirt was from the United States. Ena Hideyo, a Japanese woman with a height of 5'6, was in a white button-up shirt and black dress pants. She had brown eyes and silky brown hair that reached her shoulders. Akira Yami, a Japanese man who is 5'8, fit, had short, straight, black hair with red-dyed tips that reached his ears. He also had brown eyes and was known for wearing custom sweatpants and an animated shirt. Akim Vok was a 5'10 Russian man with a bulky build, white tips on his black military-style hair, gray eyes, who wore all black and white sportswear. Diana Slavik, a Russian woman who stood at 6'0, gave the appearance of being athletically toned, with long dark brown hair which was pulled back in a ponytail at the nape of her neck. She had eyes, the color of the ocean and wore black jeans with a fitted white t-shirt. Seth Ra, who was an Egyptian male, stood at 6'0. He was slightly buff with short straight black hair that stopped at his neck. His eyes were flame, orange in color. He wore black jeans and black t-shirt and gold jewelry. Isis Safiya was an Egyptian female from the African continent who stood 5'6, had a slim build, with long black hair that went down her back. Her eyes were brown, and she wore white dress pants, and a black button-down shirt. Lastly there was Dr. Hex who was surprisingly a youthful looking African

American male that stood 5'11. He was of average build and had short black hair that was cut close to the scalp. His eyes were dark brown, and he wore black dress pants and a black long-sleeved button-down shirt that was crisp from a hard press of the iron. He began by introducing himself.

"I am the dean of Hex University and a good friend of your parents. The last time I saw some of you was when you were kids. Now everyone has grown up. I know coming here is a surprise to all of you, but I asked your parents to send you to assist me in the next step to save humanity which I call Project *blight*."

The first person to speak up was Akira. "Alvis Hex, you're one of the most gifted scientists in history; my father worked for you in Japan, and I've been following your work since I was a child. It would be an honor to be a part of this project, but may I ask why you specifically need us?"

Just as Dr. Hex was about to say something else, Diana chimed in and stated, "I'll do this project as long as you make me Captain of the volleyball team!" She smiled to herself as if she had given him no choice.

Tomie chimed in next, "I'm a better player than she is, so you can't let her lead the team!"

After that comment, Tomie and Diana began to argue about who was the better player and deserved to be the next captain. While the others watched the argument Isis giggled.

"You two need to relax," Dr. Hex said, as he laughed. Dr. Hex slowly responded as he stood up and admired the photo of his wife on his desk. "I needed people your age for this project, and since I don't have any children of my own, I turned to your parents for assistance. I've known all of your parents for many years, and they're among the few people I trusted. They placed their trust in me with your lives, and I promised to keep you safe and look after you throughout your stay with me." Dr. Hex smiled and stated, "As much as I want to keep you all here, I'm sure you will all have a good time. To conduct this experiment, I must send all of you to one of my private locations in Arizona that is closed off to the general public and has everything you could possibly need."

Tomie and Diana looked at each other, then at Dr. Hex, and exclaimed, "ARIZONA!!!" with puzzled expressions.

Aside from Apollo, who was the only one who remained silent, the rest of the group started to laugh as they saw how upset Tomie and Diana were.

"I realize it's not what either of you expected. How about this, after you both return, I'll host a game in which you choose your own players, and the winner becomes captain." Tomie and Diana agreed, and Dr. Hex continued, "Even though this is a project, I will set up everything so you can feel at home and have fun."

Dr. Hex walked over to the elevator and instructed everyone to follow. When they reached the basement floor, they exited the elevator and followed Dr. Hex to the right and made their way to the end of the hallway. Before they entered the room, Seth noticed there was a sealed door at the opposite end of the hallway but didn't think too much of it. Once they entered the room, it appeared to have the ideal temperature, and the shelves were filled with a wide variety of plants, flowers, and fungi, as well as liquids in various containers.

They all moved toward a table that had a ten-count wooden cylinder holster on it as well as nine tiny glass cylinders that were each filled with a golden liquid. Dr. Hex stated, "This is *blight*, and according to my research, it will not take effect immediately after you receive the injections, and for you to activate it is still a mystery to me."

Seth started to ask Dr. Hex. "Do you simply expect us to serve as your lab rats? What do you mean it's a mystery to you?" "No, I wouldn't risk your lives and use you all like numbers,"

Dr. Hex replied. "Because of how much each one

of you mean to me, I made a promise to your parents that I would do everything in my power to look out for you all. This project could fundamentally alter humankind by helping us overcome our physical constraints," he continued, "I got this idea because we, as humans, have stopped depending on what the world provides us with, and are now dependent on all these tools and technology. After all my studies, work, and efforts, I've realized that I might need to go backward to move forward."

"As I began to learn more about the human body, as well as learn about plant life and everything else this world has to offer, I discovered that the solution to overcoming our constraints had been available all along." Dr. Hex directed their gazes around the room, pointing to various items. "Did you know some mushrooms have molecules that fit receptors in the brain and body almost like a puzzle? Fungi were among the first complex life forms on Earth, but most people are unaware of their properties. They have a substance called mycelium, which is made up of hyphae, that enables them to transmit electrical impulses, aiding in their expansion and communication." Dr. Hex looked at the group more intensely as he began to explain additional information. "I've also gained many resources from Australia. Due to its isolation from the rest of the world, people are unaware of the rare plants and animals that can be found there. After studying the plants, I was able to come up with a solution for human constraints to help with all humanity. This was done through reverse engineering and rewriting some of the properties for these plants and fungi. Thanks to the virus I developed using this technique you too will become stronger, faster, and more resilient. This virus mutates only to advance and aid humans in getting past their limitations of speed, strength, power, physical and mental health." After that long rant, Dr. Hex exhaled.

Isis then asked, "So with all of these pros, there must be cons, right?"

Dr. Hex explained, "I wouldn't know. That's part of the project but I can assure you all that it is not lethal and cannot result in death. I realize I'm asking a lot of you but..." He slowly turned around and said, "I will do everything in my power to see that you return to your families as the first advanced humans. All I need is your trust and we are pressed for time. One of my private jets should be arriving soon to transport you to Arizona, so who will go first?" Everyone looked around to see who would offer to go first,

"Ladies first?" Akim said jokingly, which made the other guys in the group laugh and agree.

"Well, I am a leader, so let me show you all how it's done," Diana said as she took the initiative.

While maintaining direct eye contact with Tomie she followed Dr. Hex's instructions.

"Just turn around and lift your hair. The same goes for everyone else. This injection will have to be inserted at the bottom of your neck. I'll just wipe the area with an alcohol wipe," Dr. Hex said as he approached a shelf and grabbed some wipes and a container.

He began with Diana. When he was finished, he took out the needles, and reached for a *blight* cylinder. Everyone lined up and received their injections by following the same procedure.

Tomie went next, as she said, "All right, now it's my turn. Given that she can do it, it can't be that terrifying."

Then Ena went, she asked, "What's Arizona like?"

"It's a surprise, but I promise you'll like it," Dr. Hex responded with a smile.

At that moment his phone rang. He answered, "Hello? Oh, okay, perfect timing... great." When he hung up, he looked at everyone and said, "All right, the jet is coming, so we will have to make our way to the back of the school. We still have some time, so if you have any questions or need to use the restroom before leaving, but we must do so right away." Most of the group went to the bathroom, but Apollo stayed back to talk to Dr. Hex.

"I wasn't expecting everything to move this quickly, and I don't have the luxury of leaving New Jersey, I need to help my mom with the house and my siblings. My dad is always trying to find more work nowadays, and my mom is stuck with work, along with my little brother and sister, so I usually help where I can, and I also work to help make it easier for them."

Dr. Hex placed his hand on Apollo's shoulder and said, "You're a good kid. I honestly wouldn't be here if she hadn't pushed me to stay on my path, so now I'm in a position to help her." Dr. Hex gave Apollo a hug and said, "I wish she had told me earlier, but no need to worry anymore." Apollo felt relieved and as though a weight had lifted from his shoulders. Dr. Hex let go and reached for his hand, "Now I want you to focus on this project, and don't forget to have fun and enjoy yourself, you've earned it."

Apollo shook his hand, which led to another hug. "I appreciate it. This means a lot to me."

"I'll do everything in my power to do right by you all and your families," Dr. Hex responded. Seth, who had returned earlier, lingered by the door, and listened in on Dr. Hex and Apollo's conversation.

They all made their way to the elevators and then to the back of the school. They walked up to a sizable lot with a helicopter and jet landing area, smooth black concrete ground, and a stunning view of the sky.

"This is the first time I've ever seen anything like this, especially for a college," Apollo said.

Everyone else nodded in agreement, and Akim added, "Yea, this is pretty cool."

"Yea, I pretty much live here most of the time because I also do most of my work here between all of us, this college is just a cover-up," Dr. Hex laughed. "I didn't want to draw too much attention to myself while working, so I disguised myself as one of the best schools. That, however, is unimportant."

"Mr. Hex, I'll keep an eye on Tomie and Diana for you" Isis added.

"And I can't emphasize this enough, have fun and relax and stay in touch with me. Almost forgot, here are two of my cards; everything ought to be there, but if you ever need anything, just use my cards," Dr. Hex said as he chuckled a little. He then handed Tomie the cards and said, "Just be sensible with the spending. I have to continue my research here, so remember this is very important for humanity's next step, be sure to do your best, and stay safe." Dr. Hex took another look at the group. "Look after each other."

After everyone-settled in, the pilot began preparing for takeoff. As the jet accelerated,

Apollo clenched his fists in discomfort.

"Relax a bit, it's like a rollercoaster, we'll be in the air in no time," Ena said, who was the closest to him.

After ascending to the sky, Apollo gazed at the stunning colors of the sun through the clouds, which brought him some peace. They all took a moment to reflect on Dr. Hex and how important this project was to him. They all agreed to rely on his word and to work as a unit, a family, to the best of their abilities. Halfway through the flight, Tomie and Akira were eating snacks, playing games, laughing, and going back and forth when Diana asked Isis, "So, how is Egypt, and what do you do over there?"

Isis happily replied, "Egypt is beautiful. I've lived there my entire life, and I attended medical courses, helping the poor or people in need when I had the time. I've been out of the country before, but only to accompany my mother on business trips. How about you? If I remember correctly, he said you were from Russia. What were you doing before you came over here? You obviously have a great passion for volleyball."

Diana nodded, "Russia is the motherland, she chuckled, it's really cold over there, but you get used to it. In high school, I played all kinds of sports, but volleyball is my favorite. That's why I was excited when my mother told me about Hex

University, the top college volleyball team in the country, computer science, and so much more. I'm just here for volleyball."

Akim was sound asleep next to one of the windows as they carried on their conversation. Apollo was texting his mother, asking her how his siblings were doing and letting her know what a nice man Dr. Hex was.

Ena asked Seth, "What kind of family do you have and where are you from?"

He turned away from the window and said, "I'm from Egypt, and I don't like to mention my family very much, but I'm from the royal family of Ra."

Ena retorted, "I suppose that's something we both have in common; I don't talk about my family much either, but I'm from a family of royalty as well, the Hideyo family, and I'm from Japan."

In disbelief, Seth said, "My father has mentioned the Hideyo family in the past; I never imagined this would be how I would run into one of you."

"I could say the same to you, Dr. Hex appears to have a lot of connections" Ena chuckled.

"Well, he is a talented and wealthy scientist. I guess at some point you would have a lot of connections," Seth said, as he looked back out the window.

After some time had passed Tomie, Akira, and the others passed out. Apollo was the only one who was awake. He was still in awe as he gazed out the window. The pilot woke the rest of them up as they got close to Arizona and let everyone know they would be landing in five minutes.

Havasupai, Arizona

Once they landed, the pilot assisted everyone in getting off the jet. They immediately felt the heat, sunlight, and dry air when they stepped outside. The landscape transformed into a desolate, dry area with sparse, dry trees. Diana and Akim, who were not used to the weather, began to complain.

"Why is it so hot?" Diana asked as she shaded her face from the sun.

The weather in Arizona is typically this way throughout the entire year, the pilot explained. Apollo complained about the heat, saying he'd rather it be cold. They took a short walk down this hill with carved steps that lead to their destination.

"And here you are, Arizona Havasupai, the Pilot said in a welcoming speech to the group, one of Dr. Hex's private areas that he bought out and customized for you."

The group was shocked once more with Dr.

Hex's skill. Although the area was surrounded by trees, a pleasant breeze came from the pool with the waterfall and the rocks surrounding it. A volleyball net and sandbox sparring area were set up on the opposite side, along with the three-story matte-black building embedded into the canyon wall. Everyone walked around and admired the surroundings as they made their way to the front door of the house.

The pilot led the group inside the structure, which had an interior that was made of black and white marble. The floor was covered in patterns made of cream glow stones that were also embedded in the walls. The pilot took them on a tour of the house. The kitchen, which was to the left of the entrance, had a long marble countertop in the middle and enough black chairs for everyone. The living room was located on the other side of the kitchen and had a black carpet floor, theater lights in the ceiling, a large smart TV built into the wall, as well as a PS5 and XBOX setup for entertainment. Three couches were in the room, two of which are on opposite ends and the largest of which faced the television. After moving past that area, they entered a long, well-lit hallway that leads to a gym with all the exercise machines they could possibly need and a full wall of mirrors. Before taking them to the top floor, the pilot showed them the basement, which was stocked with tools and outdoor supplies, as well as a wall that displayed specially made machetes, polearms, katanas, bows, and knives. The opposite wall was covered in guns, ranging from handguns to various assault rifle models.

"What did we just walk into? Why are all these weapons here?" Apollo questioned the pilot.

"I guess when you have a lot of money, you can really do whatever you want," Akim added.

In agreement, the pilot nodded and said, "Now let's go up to the second floor."

The woman's living quarters were located here. Each room had a queen-sized bed with black and white sheets and blankets, as well as the same black carpet and marble design. There was a television mounted on the wall, a desk with supplies, and a closet full of black, Hex-branded shirts, as well as a lot of black sweatpants and shorts. While the women settled in, the Pilot led all the men to the third floor, where their rooms were located. After showing them around, the pilot gave them time to settle in. Apollo sat on his bed, looking around, thinking to himself. *It all seemed unreal.*

After everyone had settled in, the pilot called them all into the living room and said, "I hope you all enjoy your stay. Dr. Hex has left a car, along with an SUV, in the garage near the landing zone for emergencies only. Other than that, everything here is at your disposal."

Everyone was happy with everything they had already agreed to, except for Tomie who asked, "What if we wanted to order food or something?"

The pilot quickly apologized, explaining, "You would tell them to deliver it to the landing zone, because this place is off limits to the public."

Once everyone appeared to be satisfied, the pilot instructed them to contact Dr. Hex and then left.

Seth grabbed the remote and pressed the call button, waiting for him to pick up as they heard the television ring.

"Hello, team. How was the flight, and how do you like the location?"

Everyone had a lot to say and complimented the location on its beauty both inside and out. While they were speaking, Dr. Hex simply smiled, pleased that they were less tense and more comfortable.

"I'm glad you all like the area," Dr. Hex said. "After researching all of you, I tried my best to have the area constructed to your liking."

Everyone thanked Dr. Hex and expressed their appreciation. Dr. Hex asked them to form a group so he could take a photo because he was glad to see they were more relaxed. They surrounded the couch that was facing the TV, with the shorter people positioned in front except for Seth, who stared at the others with a sense of peace, Diana made a peace sign behind Isis and Akira's heads as everyone smiled and laughed.

After they finished talking to Dr. Hex Diana asked, "Is there anything else you wanted to talk about?"

Dr. Hex responded, "Not really, just wanted to check in to make sure you all made it safely, and to remind you all to have fun, keep me updated on the progress, and most importantly, take care of each other."

Ena asked, "We still have no idea how to use the *blight*. Where do we even begin?"

Everyone else agreed because they had no idea how to activate *blight*.

Dr. Hex responded, "I know I'm asking a lot of you already, but this is also information I can't give you because I don't know the answer. My best guess is that you will activate it on your own. For the time being, just relax and keep me informed. If anything, new occurs please get in touch with me right away."

As Dr. Hex ended the call, the group said their goodbyes, and Seth began to speak in a lower tone, "Face them with annihilation, and they will survive; put them in a deadly situation, and they will live; When people fall into danger, they are then able to strive for victory... Sun Tzu, a dynasty that my father looked into. What if that is our answer to activating the *blight*?"

"Don't you think that's a little dramatic, I'm sure there could be other ways," Isis replied.

Apollo agreed nervously while smiling, "Yeah, I don't want to be plunged into a deadly situation."

Seth responded, "I didn't mean it literally, but we should do some form of sparring. Who has taken any fighting classes or knows any form of martial arts?"

Except for Isis, everyone raised their hands, and Ena remained strangely silent.

Seth said, "Well, we are just settling in today, so I don't think anyone is really in the mood to do much."

Everyone agreed that sparring could take place the next day.

"Well, it's already five o'clock. Does anyone know what we're going to do for dinner?" Tomie asked.

Diana retorted, "Yeah, I'm starving. What do we have in the kitchen?"

While some of them relaxed in the living room, Tomie and Diana went to the kitchen to see what they had. They noticed everything they could possibly need while looking around, including seasoning, rice, pasta varieties, beef, chicken, fruits, and vegetables. With this many supplies, Diana remarked, "We have everything here; we won't need to leave this place for a few months."

With a nod of agreement, Tomie said, "Right, but who really feels like cooking right now?"

Tomie made a smug face and said, "We do have Dr. Hex's cards. We can get pizza or something for the night."

Diana added to Tomie's scheme, "Sounds good. We should get chicken as well, with breadsticks, and see what toppings everyone wants."

Tomie was already searching for good pizza places that deliver. She said, "I'll get one with extra pepperoni and some barbecue chicken, and you can check in on everyone else for me."

In response, Diana said, "Sounds good, I'll take what you're getting, just make sure you get ranch on the side." Diana entered the living room and asked, "Hey guys, we're ordering food from a pizza place. Do you know what you want?"

Seth replied, "I'll take whatever, just make sure you get garlic bread sticks."

"Can you order a supreme pizza with buffalo wings and blue cheese?" Apollo replied.

Isis and Akim agreed that they'd eat whatever

everyone else ordered. "Noted, noted, and got it. Ummm... where's Ena?" Diana asked.

Seth said that Ena had gone outside for a while. When Diana stepped outside, she noticed Ena standing alone, admiring the colorful sunset, and enjoying the gentle breeze that came and went.

"Hey, we're ordering from a pizza place; do you want anything specific, and is everything okay?" Diana asked.

Ena turned around and responded, "Yea, I'll take one with sausage topping, and yes, I was just taking in the beauty of this place. It's so peaceful and lovely."

"This whole setup is amazing," Diana said.

"Maybe we can get everyone to come outside and start a fire while we eat."

Ena and Diana walked back in, and Diana gave Tomie the order details. When Tomie called, she gave them the card information and a generous tip, as well as directions to where they could drop off the food. Before the food was delivered, Diana told everyone that she would start a campfire near the sandbox area so they could eat dinner outside. They seemed to like the idea of sitting under the stars while they enjoyed a good meal. After some time, the food arrived, so Seth accompanied Apollo to retrieve everything, while the others gathered supplies from the house to start a campfire. On the walk back Apollo started talking, "you know I've never experienced stuff like this before."

With a sad glance on his face, Seth just listened to Apollo. "I also never left my hometown or even been on a plane. I'm used to working and trying to support my family as much as I can. Now all of a sudden, I'm in Arizona, helping a rich scientist, along with meeting new people that I can soon call my friends."

"I'll be glad to call you my friend as well," Seth agreed.

When they returned with the food, they saw everyone laughing and talking around the fire. They arranged all the boxes and containers on the table, next to the juices and sodas that were already there. Diana stood up in the middle of everyone as they ate and raised her cup, to state, "TO THE FUTURE OF HUMANITY, AND MOST IMPORTANTLY TO NEW FRIENDS! We will find out how to use and control the *blight*, and we will succeed."

As they raised their soda cups, the others stood up and yelled, "TO NEW FRIENDS!"

As they sat and finished their food, they continued to talk amongst themselves. Once they finished and settled down, they all laid on the ground and stargazed as they listened to the nearby waterfall and campfire crackle and enjoyed the warm sand on their backs. After a while, Ena started to clean, and Akira joined her, while the others put out the fire and brought the supplies back inside. Diana picked up Isis like a ragdoll after realizing she had fallen asleep. When Diana finally arrived in Isis' room, she dropped her on the bed, and tucked her in. As she did so, she made eye contact with Isis, and the two of them awkwardly stared at each other. Isis smiled as she held the blanket, and said, "I appreciate it, you're so strong to carry me all the way to my room."

Diana, a little flustered and speechless, stammered, "Y-You were awake this whole time!"

"I woke up after you picked me up, but since you were already planning on carrying me to my room, I pretended to be sleep so I didn't have to walk," Isis giggled, patting the empty spot on her bed. "If you want to sleep here tonight."

Diana stormed out. Her face was almost completely red, and rushed to her room, unable to say anything. While the others settled into their rooms, Apollo wandered off to the gym to use the time to exercise and reflect. He thought to himself, while bench pressing and curling, *I can't allow myself to fail. Dr. Hex is such a good person and means well. I'll figure out how to control this thing he calls blight and assist him in moving on to a better humanity.*

Chapter II

AMBITION

The next morning, Isis was in the kitchen, scrambling eggs, with onions and peppers. One could hear the sound of sausage and bacon sizzle as it was cooked on the stove. The smell permeated the air. Akim and Akira made their way downstairs around the same time.

"I wonder who's cooking right now, it smells delicious." Akira said as his mouth filled with water.

"Yeah, I'm starving and can't wait to eat."

As they approached the kitchen, they noticed Isis was cooking, while Apollo, Diana, Ena, and Tomie were already eating.

"Come on you two, it's time to eat up. We've got a long day ahead of us. If you want toast, just throw your own bread in the toaster; everything else is on the stove," Isis said.

After thanking her for breakfast, Akim and Akira took the food and sat at the table with the others.

Tomie asked, "Has anyone seen Seth? He's

missing out on breakfast."

Isis looked around, "Now that you mention it, he has been M.I.A. the whole morning, he may still be sleeping."

Akira stopped stuffing his face to say, "No, I saw him earlier this morning when I went to get something to snack on. He told me he would be in the gym."

Isis said, "I see, I will put a plate to the side for him."

With everyone else settled at the table, Isis made her plate and took a seat with everyone else. While Isis was distracted by the conversations at the table, Akira silently made his way to the last portion of food, thinking no one would notice. As the room grew silent, Akira snuck what was left of the food and Isis caught him while he stuffed his face.

She said, "Hey, you've already had your share, we're supposed to save some for Seth!"

Everyone laughed, and Akira rubbed the back of his head with a smile. "I'll make amends with him."

After they ate, they took the time to relax as they waited for Seth before they made their way outside.

Diana asked, "So we really are gonna' fight it out like some wild animals?"

Akim responded, "It sounds a bit dramatic, but he may be on to something. Humans truly don't know the true extent of their power until they are pushed into a corner."

Seth walked into the kitchen and cut off Akim and said, "And from there you choose flight, or fight." Seth smiled as he continued to speak, "and in some cases you won't have the option to flee. So, when you're left to fight, you'd be surprised at what you are capable of, when your heart is racing, and you have nothing but adrenaline running through your system." Seth made his way to the door leading outside, and said, "Let's give it a shot."

They stepped outside to the sparring sandbox wearing the shirts and shorts that Hex provided them with after everyone had some time to relax. The day was warm but there were plenty of clouds blocking the sun and a pleasant breeze, making it a good day for sparring.

"We should break it down by experience," Tomie suggests.

Seth quickly disagreed, saying, "We should divide it into boys vs. boys and girls vs. girls."

"You think you guys are stronger than us?" Tomie and Diana asked Seth.

"No, I didn't mean it that way," Seth responded, "but men are naturally stronger than women when it comes to humans."

Seth and Tomie were engaging in a stare-down while standing directly in front of each other.

Tomie said, "I'm fighting you first; watch as I lay you on your ass and force you to beg."

Seth smirked "I mean, I might like that," Seth replied.

Tomie became flustered and backed away as the others laughed, "N-No, FIGHT ME!"

"I do believe it would be a bit unfair," Apollo agreed with Seth.

Diana quickly chimed in, "I'll fight you while she fights Seth, and if we win or you forfeit, you guys have to do whatever we say for a week."

Seth and Apollo exchanged glances. "Sounds like a deal, but if we win, you girls have to do whatever we say for a week."

Diana and Tomie accepted the proposal. Isis and Akira exchanged a look of *what the hell did we get ourselves into, I didn't want any part of this.* Akira face-palmed himself.

Everyone nodded in agreement as Isis announced the rules, "No cheap shots, and everyone must pull their punches. Even though we made a deal, we aren't here to hurt each other." Isis continued, "The first fight will be Akim vs Ena, followed by Diana vs Apollo, and lastly Seth vs Tomie. While me and Akira are the refs."

Isis counts down, "3...2...1...FIGHT!" as Akim takes a boxing stance and Ena takes a defensive counter stance. Akim shuffled in the sand towards Ena and threw the first punch, missing as Ena dodged, she grabbed him under his arm and into a Supplex position, then slammed him on his back.

Akim was taken by surprise and quickly recovered, he bounced back into his stance. "I didn't expect you to be so quick, so I'll stop holding back." Akim stated.

Ena went on the offensive, swinging left and right before launching a tornado kick that was blocked by Akim. When she threw the tornado kick, he grabbed her leg and dragged her closer, using his size advantage to prepare to slam her.

"COME ON ENA, YOU GOT THIS!" Diana encouraged her.

Ena was quick enough, to wrap her legs around his neck. She spun around and threw him to the ground again. Akim rolled in the sand and stood up, spitting the sand out of his mouth, thinking, *She's probably faster and smarter than me, but I need to use my size to my advantage.* The girls continue to root for Ena, while the guys tell Akim to take his time and get his shit together. He inhaled deeply before returning to his boxing stance.

Ena, being respectful, asked, "Alright, are you

ready?"

Akim replied, "Yea, let's finish this."

Ena went on the offensive again and charged right at him. While Akim prepared to attack, she went in for a diving kick. Akim took it to the chest, grabbed her by the leg, and threw her back using only his brute strength. He gave her very little time to stand up as she rolled around in the sand. He then proceeded to throw an axe kick. Ena was quick enough to push off the ground and into a backflip. She recovered faster than he expected. Akim's pursuit came to a halt, resulting in a stare down between him and Ena, with everyone remaining silent except for the sound of the waterfall in the distance and the wind that was blowing through the trees. A leaf slowly passed between them, and as soon as it hit the sand, they both charged at one another. Ena saw that Akim was overextending when he delivered a left punch. Using her speed to her advantage, she dodged to her right, snuck up behind him, jumped on his back, and put him in a choke hold. Akim eventually tapped out as he sank to one knee while still clinging to her arm after he realized she had him in a tight chokehold. Ena unwrapped herself from Akim, and Isis crowned Ena the winner and raised her hand. Akim sat in the sand, stunned at how quickly he lost, as Tomie and Diana cheered Ena on. Ena helped Akim up, and they both smiled as they shook hands and said, "Good fight."

They moved to the side, while Apollo and Diana took their respective sides of the sandbox. Isis stood in the center, ready to count down, while Diana assumed her fighting stance and Apollo nervously raised his fist.

Shaking his head, Seth predicted the fight wouldn't last longer than ten seconds, considering Diana's overwhelming confidence, and from the unsure look in Apollo's eyes. "3...2...1...FIGHT!" Isis said.

Diana smiled, already sensing Apollo's frailty, as if she were a predator stalking prey. He moved in a few steps as Diana charged at him. She kicked him with a left kick that he blocked, this prompted her to follow it with a quick right kick that hit him because he didn't see it coming. To seal the deal, she tornado kicked Apollo face first into the ground. She left Apollo curled up in the sand and shocked everyone with how badly she beat him.

"What a fight, since it's two to zero for the girls there would be no point in this last fight," Isis exclaimed as she declared Diana the winner.

Seth interrupted her mid-sentence. "I want to fight Diana and Tomie at the same time, and if I win, the bet is off since it will count as a draw."

Tomie laughed and said, "If those two couldn't

beat us one on one, why do you think you have a chance?"

"No offense, but I'm not Apollo or Akim," Seth said as he walked to his side of the sandbox. "This will be a testament to my strength. So, don't hold back."

Tomie and Diana took their place in the sandbox, and said, "I guess we'll have to beat your conceited ass until you surrender."

Everyone else was on the sidelines as Isis returned to the center to count down the fight.

"Alight, this is the moment that will decide everything; if Seth wins, the deal is off. And if the girls win, haha, we got plans for you," Isis said with a smug expression.

While Diana took a stance that resembled that of a kickboxer, she let Tomie go first. Isis started the countdown with "3...2...1...fight" Tomie went on the attack and threw left and right jabs, crosses, and hooks, and Seth grinned as he dodged each hit. He grabbed her by the collar, drew her in, and delivered a direct kick to her stomach. Tomie, slid on all fours, stopped herself and stood up.

"Hey, is that all you got?" Seth mocked her.

Tomie takes another stance, "I underestimated you; it won't happen again."

"I warned you not to hold back, and more or

less never underestimate your opponent." Seth said, appearing somewhat agitated.

Seth started to punch left and right as they both inched closer to each other. Tomie, who had no trouble dodging and blocking, when she noticed a gap after Seth threw-a right hook. She pushed his left arm back with her left hand before striking him in the stomach with a punch that was followed by a left hook to the jaw.

Before she could finish, Seth grabbed her arm and said, "Gotta hit harder than that," and clipped her before backing away gaining distance. "Listen, I know we're just practicing, but when you're fighting me, don't hold back. Hit me as hard as you need to and fight me as you see fit."

Diana rushed up to Seth and said, "You said it, not me."

Diana landed a slew of punches and kicks that he struggled to deflect. As soon as Tomie stood up, she pushed her hair out of her face and blindsided Seth by delivering a sidekick to his face, which knocked him to the sand.

"There you go, now we can get started," Seth said with a smile. Seth got up and took a firm stance, ready to fight, while Diana and Tomie took their stances side by side. He used the come at me taunt, which caused Diana to charge first. Seth blocked Diana's left kick, but the force pushed him back. Tomie followed up with a combination of punches that Seth struggled to keep up with as he wondered *how much she was holding back*.

"NOW IT'S MY TURN" Diana yelled and charged in from the side with an axe kick, which forced Tomie to shift back, as Seth blocked it with both arms, it forced him to one knee. Seth pushed Diana back, which caused her to fall on her back, while Tomie followed up with a dropkick. Seth didn't have time to react, so Tomie's kick sent him sliding, but he recovered quickly. Diana rushed Seth, and threw punches left and right, which forced Seth to shift back and dodge all her hits. Tomie rushed in from the side again as Seth threw a sweep kick, that caused Diana to fall, and guard him from Tomie's punches. Seth went on the offensive, throwing kicks and punches that forced Tomie to be on defense. Diana re-entered the fight. She hooked Seth in the jaw and caused him to stumble back. Seth smiled, as if he enjoyed himself.

"Ready to give up yet? You can't defeat us," Tomie stated.

They were all sweating and exhausted.

"No, this is the part that I like the most. My blood is pumped, and I don't get this feeling enough," Seth replied.

Diana and Tomie smiled, "I guess we're all on

the same page. The fights not over until one of us stays down."

Tomie added, "Right, and stop pulling your punches. You asked for a fight, so give us the same effort."

Seth nodded, "So the real fight begins now."

Diana charged in and delivered a front kick to the chest. Seth slid back into the sand and his smile turned into a glare. He blocked Diana's right hook with his left arm and pushed her back as he stood up again. He wiped the sand off his face, and took an orthodox stance, taunting them to fight. This time, Diana took the initiative, and launched a left-handed punch that Seth countered, then he punched her in the stomach. Diana threw a right hook, which he blocked with his left arm as he pushed her back. Tomie now led the assault and threw a left feint punch which made Seth flinch and cover his face. She grinned, as she followed up with a heavy right hook, and passed his weak attempt to guard as she hit him in the jaw. While he fought Tomie, Seth caught a glimpse of Diana as she tried to sneak up behind him and he threw a reverse kick which sent her back. Then he proceeded to throw a weak left jab at Tomie's face that she tried to block but he smiled as he switched to a heavy straight right punch to the chest. Tomie was in pain, but she reacted quickly. She grabbed his arm and hurled him to the ground. Next, she squeezed him into an arm bar.

"GIVE IT UP TAP OUT!" Tomie yelled.

Not wanting to give up, Seth used his raw strength to try to get up while holding Tomie's hands together to prevent her from breaking his arm. Diana rushed back and attempted to put an end to the fight. Seth closed his eyes and used all his willpower to try to think of a way out of this terrible situation. Everything happened in slow motion. He closed his eyes and thought, *am I really going to lose here? I'm so exhausted. I am. UNBREAKABLE! I am... UNSTOPPABLE!*

When Seth finally opened his eyes, the iris of his eyes shone bright shades of purple almost like the nebulas in space, and total darkness crept into the white outer layer of his eye like a black hole swallowing the light. The sudden change in pressure caught Tomie and Diana off guard for a moment. Seth then swung Tomie off his arm, expending a mysterious energy that caused her to slide across the sandbox. Everyone was speechless, and Diana was too frightened to carry on fighting. Apollo and Akim moved between Seth and Diana as Isis sprinted over to check on Tomie.

Apollo's speech was slurred, "A- Alright the fight is over!"

Seth smirked as he made eye contact with Apollo. "I suppose I've won this round."

Seth's eyes caught Apollo's attention, as he watched Seth's sclera returning to white like the end of an eclipse, but his iris only dimmed to a dull purple and did not return to their original orange color.

"Yeah, most definitely," Apollo said nervously.

Seth sat down in the sand and took a deep breath. Everyone kept their distance from Seth on the other end of the sandbox as he said, "Finally... I'll give it to you two, I wasn't expecting you guys to put up such a fight. That's the most fun I had in a while," as he looked up at the sky and watched the clouds pass by. "What's wrong?" Seth asked as he looked around. "Why are you all so worried?"

"We think you did it, you activated your *blight*," Apollo replied. We should go see Dr. Hex."

They brushed off the sand went inside and called Dr. Hex. He answered after a few rings, "Hey guys, how's everything going, I assume you made some kind of progress to call so suddenly?"

"Yea, we think Seth may have activated his *blight* while we were sparring," Isis said hesitantly. As soon as Diana and Tomie forced him into a corner while he was in combat, he just let loose with this powerful force of energy.

"Seth, what were you thinking about for it to activate?" Dr. Hex was at a loss for words.

Apollo continued, "The whiter layer of his eyes... they turned black, with his iris changing to these interesting shades of purple. They didn't return to normal after he stopped; his white outer layer of his eyes came back to normal, but his iris appeared to be permanently purple."

Seth looked at his eyes using the camera on his phone, "Wow Dr. Hex they really are purple... I just didn't want to lose." Seth continued to peer into his eyes. He was in awe. "Losing was not an option," he said.

Dr. Hex paused for a moment to consider the possible cause. "It appears to have been triggered by your ambition."

As Dr. Hex spoke, Tomie walked across the room to the kitchen to get bottled water for everyone. *This is so unexpected* Dr. Hex thought to himself. He asked, "But wouldn't this also mean Tomie or Diana had an opportunity to activate theirs? There are probably more factors that we have overlooked, but I am pleased with the quick results. I'll also take a look at the video feed." After giving out water to everyone, Tomie yelled "think fast" as she threw a bottle at Seth's face. Seth was hit in the face by a water bottle that fell into his lap because he didn't react quickly enough. Diana laughed and asked,

"You're mad that you got your ass kicked-"

"Didn't you fail to beat Seth, though? You were fighting alongside her," Apollo said, interrupting the conversation.

Tomie and Diana stared at Apollo, who nervously smiled and looked away, as he said, "never mind."

They returned their attention to the main topic at hand.

"So far I don't have much information to go off of," Dr. Hex said as he finished typing notes, "but this is more progress than nothing, and early results that were unexpected. Thank you for your effort, and please keep me informed of any changes. I'll now need daily updates from Seth." Seth nodded. "For everyone else, it might be a different approach, or it might take more time, so don't feel like you're failing in any way, this is part of the project, just keep me informed and have fun," he said and waved goodbye. Everyone waved back and the television screen went dark. Most of the team chose to relax on their own terms and went to their rooms after the long day.

The bruises and cuts Seth sustained during the fight had completely disappeared by the time he got out of the shower; it was as if they had never occurred. He then began to wipe the steam from the mirror with his hand, just enough to see his reflection. He couldn't stop staring at his purple-colored eyes. On the other hand, Tomie laid in her room and stared up at the ceiling. She refused to concede to defeat.

Diana came downstairs to the smell of chicken and rice after some time and proceeded to take a seat at the black marble counter, while she watched Isis cook, shuffling back and forth from the counter to the stove.

Diana asked, "What are you cooking up this time?"

"Decided to make Lemon chicken and rice, with peppers, onions, and some fresh cut fries on the side," Isis said after pausing for a moment.

Diana decided to get up and assist with the preparation after observing her move back and forth so quickly and with such ease. Diana said, "You don't have to do all the work alone. Even though I don't cook frequently, I'll try to help if you give me the right instructions."

"After you wash your hands, grab two peppers of each color, red, green, and yellow, and I'll show you how to cut them. The rice, chicken, and fries will be almost done after we finish sautéing the peppers, so the meal should be ready soon." Isis said as she smiled and nodded.

Diana gathered the supplies Isis requested from the fridge and she began to wash the peppers before beginning to cut them step by step, she then instructed Diana to do the same with the rest of them.

Diana asked, "Why didn't you join the session today?" while cutting the peppers. "You already know that eventually you'll need to participate in some activities with us to learn more about this virus and what makes it tick."

Isis said, "I don't have it in me to fight; my job is to take care of people; I've wanted to help people since I was old enough to remember, she continued, I could never muster the energy to fight or harm someone else."

Diana responded, "So you've never had to defend yourself or fight for anything your entire life?"

Isis replied, "No... even if I did, I'd rather run or avoid the situation. I don't believe that fighting or harming someone is ever the solution to any problem."

Diana became agitated and said, "You can't have that kind of mindset, you need to learn how to at least defend yourself, this world is full of disgusting people."

Isis replied with a smile. "And that's why I try to be as kind as possible, Have you ever heard that hurt people just hurt people?" Diana nodded as Isis continued, "so if that chain never breaks, there will be a bunch of people projecting the same energy they received and they will pass that negative energy on. That's why I try my best to be kind and help where I can. One kind gesture, no matter how small or large, can change someone's perspective, and now we can have people helping others, hopefully changing the flow of things." Diana was finished with the peppers and placed them in a bowl, and she found herself more open to Isis' perspective.

Diana responded, "You have a point, but that doesn't give you the right to be naive and disregard knowing how to defend yourself." Diana thought to herself for a moment and came up with a solution, "How about I teach you how to defend yourself while you teach me more about your perspective?"

Isis replied with a smile. "Sounds fair."

When the food was ready, Isis told everyone to get their plates and eat. While they made their way downstairs. The pleasant smell of the lemon chicken rice, and peppers seeped through the atmosphere. Akira and Akim were the first to arrive at the table, followed by everyone else, who all thanked Isis for another home cooked meal. The group began to eat and talk. After they finished eating, they parted ways and went to their rooms to rest after a long day. Tomie tossed and turned, not being able to sleep. She got up and went to Seth's room. She knocked on his door until he woke up. He peeked through the door after a brief delay and, upon seeing

Tomie he asked, "It's the middle of the night; what could you possibly want?"

"I need you to fight me," Tomie said, glaring at him. "I can't sleep, and I'm not going to let the fight end the way it did."

Seth stood there, his hair a mess, speechless, he replied, "So you woke me up... so you can get your ass beat again, this couldn't have waited 'til tomorrow?"

Tomie, even more irritated, responded, "I won't let you win, just get outside so I can have my rematch." Seth realized that Tomie would not leave him alone until they fought. He put on some clothes and went outside. The sound of a waterfall could be heard in the distance as they stepped outside into the warm, comforting air. They each took a position in the sandbox, and Tomie declared the ground rules: "No dirty tricks, no holding back, and no stopping until the other person admits defeat." Seth nodded in agreement. They moved cautiously in the sand as they approach one another, Tomie saw that he was waiting for her to approach, rushed in launching the initial assault. She landed two deliberate left head jabs that forced him to cover his face before landing a powerful right hook to the stomach. Seth, who was not particularly affected, threw a right hook that Tomie tried to block by raising one arm, but she underestimated the force and slid in the sand while she attempted to defend herself. *Why does my arm feel numb if he only attacked once?* she thought as she tried to defend herself against Seth's assault, he swung left and right which caused her to shift backwards step by step. She let her guard down briefly from the fatigue she felt in her arms, which allowed Seth to deliver a powerful tornado kick to her left arm, knocking her into the sand. Seth told Tomie, who was covered in sand and bruises, to "stay down, you can't win."

"No, this fight is far from over," Tomie said as she struggled to look up and saw his purple eyes under the moonlight. *Why is he so powerful...* At that moment Tomie stood up again in front of Seth and refused to back down.

Tomie said, "I've already told you that I'm not going to lose; you can knock me down as many times as you want, but you'll be the one to tap out first." Tomie avoided a right hook from Seth by shoulder tackling him to the ground as she pounced on top of him and swung repeatedly.

While Seth shielded his face from her punches, he let his guard down and took a punch to the face, which allowed him to grab one of her wrists. Tomie attempted to swing with the other arm, and Seth was able to grab her other wrist. Tomie was tired, short of breath, and irritated as she struggled to break free from Seth's grip.

"It's okay, you can't beat me," Seth said softly, now speaking with concern in his voice, I'm sure you've noticed that even if the *blight* isn't active, just unlocking it has made me stronger."

Tomie became agitated and struggled even more. Her sclera slowly turned black, like the sun being eclipsed, and her iris became a brilliant purple, resembling the colors in space.

"I AM NOT WEAK, AND I AM NOT ALLOWED TO BE WEAK... IMMA SHOW YOU HOW STRONG I AM... IMMA, SHOW EVERYONE HOW STRONG I AM!"

Tomie finally broke free from his grip and began to throw punches, while Seth tried to shield his face from being hit. When he saw the opportunity, he kicked her in the back and stood up, returning to his stance, waiting for Tomie to make a move. Seth noticed Tomie's eyes and thought *what is this pressure, is this the same thing that happened to me?*

When she got up, she flicked her hair back and said, "You look scared. Don't give up now, the fight is just beginning,"

Her eyes are exactly as they described mine, and her entire demeanor has changed.

Tomie oozed with confidence as she said. "I'll end this properly now!"

Seth was surprised by the force of Tomie's fast

right flying kick, which he blocked by covering the left side of his face with one arm. The kick sent him out of the sandbox. Seth held his rib cage while he coughed up blood. *The blight's power is... incredible.* Tomie moved toward Seth as she came from the sandbox.

With pain in her voice, she said to Seth, "Now nobody can bully me around anymore, not even you!"

When he heard the pain in her voice and recognized that the anger came from somewhere else, he slowly rose and admitted defeat as he hugged her.

"You win," Seth said. I'm not sure what you've been through, but you're a fighter. I haven't looked down on you since we met."

Tomie slowly hugged him back and shed a few tears as her sclera gradually returned to white and her iris turned a dim purple color. It took her a moment to feel his heartbeat and warm embrace.

"Thank you."

Tomie passed out from the awakening of her blight, Seth walked away with Tomie on his shoulder as he held his rib cage. When he arrived at her room, he plopped her on the bed and gazed at her as she slept peacefully. Seth struggled to make his way to the living room, where he sat on the couch and dialed Dr. Hex.

He answered the phone and asked, "Is everything all right?" Dr. Hex looked up and noticed Seth was hurt. "What happened, it looks like you were hit by a truck!"

Seth replied with a weak voice, "Yea, I just finished sparring with Tomie. So, I guess she is the equivalent. I couldn't get any sleep because she wouldn't let me until she had a rematch. She also awakened her Blight toward the end of the session, and it appears that one way for it to awaken is out of rage or ambition, as you previously mentioned.

Dr. Hex asked, "Is she okay? And did you notice anything else?"

"She fell asleep, and we both noticed physical improvements," Seth responded. "Even if it isn't activated, you are faster, stronger, and more durable than before. In addition to having a faster healing factor, when you activate the *blight*, your sclera turns black, and your iris turns purple. It also appears that once you leave that state, your sclera turns white again, but your iris remains purple, never to return to its original state."

"So, it appears to be working as it should," Dr. Hex replied, "this situation with the eyes is very interesting to me. It may be too soon to tell, but I believe this will happen to anyone who activates the *blight*. It must be the *blight* altering your DNA, nothing to worry about, as this was designed to improve human capabilities."

Seth said, "I know we all agreed to be here, and I do trust you. But why are you so sure this won't backfire? What if someone can't handle it? Or if-"

He was interrupted by Dr. Hex, who said, "I've said it before; this virus can't and won't cause death. Although I understand your skepticism, the ingredients cannot and will not backfire. I will need to do more research on the eyes, which is the only thing I can't explain to you. This virus will protect you and only make you stronger from now on."

Seth then asked, "So, if you're so sure of your work, why didn't you take it with us? Why did you require participants from all over the world for this experiment? It must be something you're not telling us."

Dr. Hex responded calmly, "I need more than one person for an experiment like this, as you noticed it's two people from each country, as well as both genders. One, I needed to see how each gender would react to the *blight*. Two, I wanted to check out any additional effects that coming from a different origin might have. Since I've made every effort to use only ingredients that the earth has to offer and avoid using any unnecessary ingredients, I'm confident that this virus won't harm any of you. I don't want any of you to feel like lab rats and remember that I sent you to one of my private locations to keep you all away from the public eye. Nobody can learn about something like this because it is still too early in the world we live in. It would only be used for the wrong reasons. If that makes you all feel better, I'll take it myself. I'll call back later today when everyone is available, try to get some rest, and thank you for the update and excellent work."

Seth made it to his room, as he still held on to his ribs. He crashed on his bed and looked at the ceiling. *What will come next* was his final thought before he drifted off to sleep.

Chapter III

TEENAGERS

Tomie awoke in a cold sweat and looked around until she figured out, she was in her bedroom. She went to the bathroom took a deep breath and immediately washed her face. She couldn't stop staring at her eyes in the mirror. *My eyes are... purple. Just like Seth, I awakened my blight,* she thought to herself. She brushed her teeth and headed downstairs to the kitchen and noticed that everyone was in the living room talking to Dr. Hex. They all stopped talking and turned to look at her; Seth was the first to speak again. "We decided to let you sleep in this morning, sleeping beauty, because you had a long-"

Isis softly mushed Seth's face before he could finish speaking and gave Tomie a warm smile. "Stop teasing her, congratulations on awakening your *blight*."

Tomie walked into the living room, greeted Dr. Hex, and caught up on the parts of the conversation she missed. Dr. Hex finally explained why he called in the first place. He began by saying, "So, after speaking with Seth last night, I never considered taking the *blight* for myself, I believed there was no need to do so. I want your complete trust and to demonstrate that you are not just subjects or lab rats." He then showed them the cylinder they were given before leaving. "I will take the *blight* as a sign of trust, and may it strengthen our bond."

Everyone watched as he injected himself into the back of his neck. After it was done Dr. Hex said, "I will also call in more frequently to keep you guys updated on my end. As I previously stated, I appreciate your effort."

He hung up, and everyone went their separate ways. Isis and Diana left the house to get some fresh air, while the others stayed in. They passed the waterfall and made their way through the trees and took advantage of the shade.

"It's impressive how quickly they've awakened the *blight*," Diana said. "I thought I'd be one of the first to use it, but I guess I was wrong."

Isis smiled and said, "I guess it works differently for all of us, but it is amazing to see progress. You put in just as much effort as those two, but you had no sign of the *blight*. We don't really understand how it operates either, so I can only assume that it will come to you when the time is right."

Diana looked over at Isis while they were walking, and watched as she smiled the same moment the sunlight slipped through the trees. Diana responded, "You're right, the day will come; I guess there's no use in beating myself up 'bout it. How do you feel about not having yours yet? I just assumed you don't care."

Isis answered, "Actually, I'd like to have it activated; I want to know how it feels, as well as the benefits of having such a virus. Imagine all the good it could do for people; what if it could treat cancer or combat viruses that we are unable to eradicate? Imagine the endless capabilities of the *blight*, that we have yet to even fathom. This is a huge leap in Human development. Diana exhibited a hint of concern as she observed how excited Isis was while discussing the topic. Isis said, "Dr. Hex could have made something that could help humanity move forward."

Diana interjected, "you're always so optimistic. What about all the people who want to watch the world burn, or all the insane people or warlords who want to use it for other purposes? There's a reason Hex hasn't shown this to anyone yet, and why we're in this private location. The *blight* cannot fall into the hands of the wrong people. You can't keep looking on the bright side of things without seeing the darkness that lurks with it."

Isis replied, "I understand that, but we can't be afraid to help people and move in unity; if we keep refusing to do so, humans will be divided and never come together again. You're here to help me avoid being so naive and defenseless; you'll teach me, and I'll teach you how we can bring people together." Diana nodded.

"HAHA, YOU CAN'T STOP ME! I AM A BEAST!" Akira said, "Alright, hand the sticks over to someone else, who's next?!"

Ena laughed; she watched as Apollo and Akim played the game. Apollo handed the controller over to Akim.

"Alright, it's time to end that streak you've been building up." Akim said.

Tomie was on her phone while Seth was outside in the hot sandbox working out and perfecting his form. Seth reflected to himself; *I shouldn't be able to train right now. Tomie put me through a tree and yet I'm able to function. The blight is incredible.* Seth eventually exited the sandbox and stood in front of a tree. He guided his fist a few times before unleashing a powerful right hook that caused the tree to cave in and eventually fall over. Seth inspected his scratched-up fist after he slammed it into the tree bark. *This isn't even the full extent of the blight's power but look at what I can accomplish with my bare hands*. When nightfall arrived, they decided to give Isis a break and spent the night eating pizza, as they talked and joked. After dinner everyone except Apollo went to their room. He remained in the gym to finish a full workout. As he swung at a punching bag, he thought to himself. *Seth and Tomie have already activated their blight; I can't afford to fall behind... Is it possible that I'm not strong enough? AM I JUST WEAK?* He threw the last round of hard punches and sat on the rubber floor. He tried to catch his breath as he wiped away the sweat. Seth and Tomie were the only ones to have their *blight* awakened in the three weeks that already passed, with only a few phone calls to Dr. Hex regarding the progress made. Even Dr. Hex has yet to activate his *blight*. However, based on the information provided, the *blight* performs exactly as Dr. Hex desired, if not better.

It's been nearly six weeks now, Seth and Tomie have been training more frequently in the last few weeks. Isis was beginning to show Diana how they can make the world a better place, as Diana taught Isis how to defend herself in combat. The others continued with the same schedule of exercising, playing games, and eating. Along with doing group activities such as volleyball, game nights, watching movies, and simply getting to know each other better. Isis decided to teach Diana how to cook breakfast

Friday morning of week six, while the rest of the group came down one by one, to the lovely, blended aroma of eggs, sausages, peppers, onions, potatoes, and bacon. Seth was the last to wake up. He struggled to breathe and woke up suddenly in a profuse sweat as he tried to catch his breath. *What is this icy sensation in my chest? It makes me feel like I just died,* Seth thought to himself. As he pushed off the covers to get out of bed, he heard a voice. It was soft like a woman.

"Seth, what a powerful name. Find me."

As strange as it was to hear that voice, Seth didn't think too long about it. He continued to get dressed and made his way to the kitchen with the rest of the group. They had already started eating. The T.V. was on in the background and provided a noise that was like white noise. The group never heard the news anchors describe the horrific events that were happening.

The newscaster said, "There have been reports of people having violent outbursts, killing, fighting, and even eating one another all over the world. They were initially thought to be fake."

The newscaster was interrupted, and someone gave her more papers while they whispered in her ear. She continued, now at a loss for words and wearing a look of complete despair.

"H-here is some of the recent footage that has been spreading of the dead coming back to life after being mutilated." They censored the video just enough so that viewers could still understand the situation. "We still have no information about the origin of the situation or how it even began," she said, "but we advise everyone to stay at home... God be with us during this difficult time."

After everyone finished eating, the girls decided to relax in the water at the base of the waterfall. Seth went about his daily practice and training regimen. The other guys prepared to cook some food outside. They set up the grill, tables, and chairs in place.

Ena said to no one in particular, "The weather is so beautiful today, we should play volleyball again. How does that sound?"

The others nodded happily in agreement.

Diana said, "Me and Tomie will be the captains and choose our team. I know you want Seth on your team, so I'll let you have him."

Tomie, stunned and stuttering, "Wha-What is that supposed to mean!"

The other girls laughed. "We've noticed how close you two have been, y'all play fight, the little back and forth talk, you two are just so cute," Diana said to tease Tomie with a smug expression on her face.

Tomie blushed a bit with her head halfway in the water. Afterward she stood up and dragged Diana into the water. She pushed her repeatedly, saying, "YOU THINK YOU'RE SO FUNNY, TAKE THIS! Don't think we're not paying attention to you and Isis!"

Ena is the only one laughed, while Isis covered her face. The sound from the water was heard by the guys.

Akim said, "I wonder what they could be talking about over there."

Akira said, "Don't waste your time trying to understand women, because women don't even understand each other."

They decided to let the girls do whatever they wanted. After they finished, they went about their business for the time being, and Apollo sought assistance from Seth.

"Hey, can you teach me how to fight? Apollo asked. I feel like I'm falling behind everyone else, and you were the first to activate your *blight*."

The wind blew gently as Seth looked at him in awkward silence. *This is very unexpected*, Seth thought. He said, "sure," in response. Apollo followed Seth as he entered the sandbox.

"You seem fit, so we can skip the exercise," Seth

said. "We'll begin with some basic sparring to see where you stand."

Apollo raised his fists in preparation for battle as he remembered the time Diana easily defeated him. Apollo told himself, *I'm not a pushover, I can handle this.*

Seth was getting ready, saying, "Alright, here I come!"

Seth rushed at Apollo. He faked a right punch that Apollo fell for. Seth, then hit him with a left hook that knocked him to the ground as he yelled, "Get up," to Apollo.

He slowly stood up, already trembling in pain, and raised his guard once more. The girls were still in the water, watching the fight between Seth and Apollo.

"I wonder what got into them, they seem to be practicing," Isis said.

Tomie continued, "Apollo has worked out in the gym more than anyone. He must think he needs to prove something."

Apollo threw a few punches, which Seth easily parried. Seth then struck back by grabbing Apollo by the collar and kicking him back into the sand. Under the scorching sun, Apollo was on his knees, as he clutched his stomach and stared up at Seth's silhouette and purple eyes. *So, this is the difference between someone like me and a user of the blight...* Apollo thought to himself. *I'll never be able to compete with him without the blight... But even before that, I couldn't compete with someone like him.* Seth extended his hand to assist Apollo.

"You need to be more confident and stop doubting your own strength," Seth said. If you keep telling yourself that you can't, you'll never get anywhere. We will continue sometime tomorrow."

"Two to two, GAME TIED NOW!" Diana screamed after landing a powerful spike that Seth couldn't dig.

Tomie's team was made up of Seth and Akira, with Seth preparing to serve. While Diana got Isis and Ena ready to receive, Akim and Apollo decided to cook burgers and hot dogs on the grill while they watched the others play volleyball. After trading points from spikes, blocks, digs, and sets, the game was nineteen to nineteen. With Akira up to serve, he served the ball just barely over the net, forcing Diana to dive for the save. Isis rushed for the set. Since she was unable to properly get under it, she bumped set it to Ena, who took her steps one, one, and two jumps and swung straight past Tomie's block from the left of the net to the right corner. Seth reacted quickly enough to get the ball in the air, Akira screamed, "I GOT IT!" for the second touch as he tried to set it. The ball slipped through his hands with the sun in his eyes, giving Diana's team the point.

Diana served the ball to Akira, who made a clean pass to Tomie, who then set it up for Seth, who spiked it right through Diana's block. Forcing Ena to block her face, which turned out to be a sloppy pass. Isis dove for the ball, sending it towards the net. When the ball was high and close enough to the net, Diana took a step back and started to jump while Tomie tried to block her. At the last second, she stopped slowly dumping the ball to score the winning point.

Diana screamed, "THAT'S HOW IT'S DONE! Wahoo!"

Tomie kneeled in the sand and held her fist, as she thought to herself *cheap ass point.* They cleaned off the sand and went over to the grill to get some food before they sat at the table. As she swiped through her phone to check her social media, Tomie munched on a cheeseburger while she watched the videos of people fight and kill one another. "Guys, have any of you checked into what's happening?" she asked. What are all these videos about?"

After Tomie passed her phone around, Akira responded, "It might just be click-bait or something, because this doesn't even look real."

A few of them nodded, and Seth added, "Yeah,

it's social media, you never know what's real or fake without an actual source."

Diana laughed a little and said, "Did you read the comments, these people can't take anything seriously, the internet will always be undefeated. If it were true, it would have made the news, and we would have heard about it by now."

They separated one by one after everyone had pushed the topic aside.

Later in the day, before the sun set, Seth and Apollo went out for more training.

Seth said, "Alright, Like I said before. Being confident is one of the steps to move forward, you also need to trust your instinct and not hesitate."

They took their respective sides as they entered the sandbox.

"I only know boxing, so I asked you to train me in other fighting styles," Apollo said.

"Not just beat you up, Seth sneered, When I first started training, I didn't know any form, and I had no idea what I was doing. My father brought me to our training rooms, and he was the first person I had to fight. Of course, I kept losing, but after a while, I started to observe him every day. I've learned everything through endurance, defeat, and being beaten nearly to death. So, I don't have much to teach you other than that failure is the key to learning, and that you should be prepared to endure whatever I throw at you." Seth bolted without warning, throwing punches left and right that Apollo deflected.

While fighting, Seth advised him, "Fight back, you can't win by only being defensive."

Seth threw a jab at his face, which he avoided, prompting Seth to grab the back of his neck with the same hand he threw a punch with. As Apollo struggled to break free, he noticed Seth prepared to attack again. For a moment, Apollo pushed him back to gain some distance. He went on the offensive and closed the gap between them. Seth avoided a jab thrown by Apollo without even trying. Then came a quick uppercut, that caused Seth to stumble back. Next Apollo launched a powerful left hook, which Seth avoided. He stooped to his right and planted his hands in the sand. Then he kicked Apollo in the ribs, which sent him tumbling in the sand.

Apollo screamed in agony, "You could at least hold back a bit, I don't have the same endurance as you."

Seth stood over Apollo and said in a raised voice, full of frustration, "Holding back is a sign of disrespect, you wouldn't learn anything from me doing so. Get up now!"

As he watched Apollo struggle, Seth clenched his teeth and thought to himself, *you people are so fucking weak.* Seth exhaled, and said, "Never mind, we will pick it up tomorrow. Try to get some rest today. You did fine." Seth returned to the house, and left Apollo in the sand. As the sun set, the sky became a stunning combination of colors, and the sound of the waterfall could be heard in the distance. Apollo eventually stood up and walked slowly back inside the house.

Apollo was the center of attention as everyone in the living room stared at him awkwardly while Akira questioned, "What happened to you?"

With a tentative smile, Apollo said, "Just finished some training with Seth. What are you all doing here?"

"We tried calling Dr. Hex, but he didn't respond, Akira replied, so, we have to wait until tomorrow."

They all went to their rooms one at a time to get some rest for the night.

Chapter IV

A BEAUTIFUL COLLAPSE

Everyone sat in the living room the following morning to figure out why Dr. Hex hadn't called. Apollo asked the others to check and see if it was just him or if they also had no cell service. Afterwards they were all silent for a few seconds after they were sure they had no access to the outside world.

Tomie said, "We need to conn-" She was cut short. The TV came on and sounded the government's emergency warning siren. What they saw next took them by surprise. There were images of dead people killing the living. While others were shown clawing at their face and gouging out their eyes.

"This footage is not fake; this is a global epidemic that has been ignored by the public. For the past three months the numbers of dead and infected people have been rising; the origin of this virus is still unknown, a stern voice instructed, despite this crisis, humanity must survive. Military aid has been sent throughout the country for the past few weeks. Stay at home wait for help, be on high alert, and be ready for anything. In these dark times, may God be with us."

For a while no one said anything as they all silently watched the footage in a state of shock.

"We have to make it to Dr. Hex," Seth said, breaking the silence. "We can't sit here any longer. We've been here while the world fell apart."

Akira asked Seth, "How are we supposed to get there? We don't have any means of communication or transportation. What if he is already dead?"

Isis added to the conversation, "He is our only hope. If he created the Blight, I'm sure he could figure out what's going on and try to help."

Tomie said, "What about the CDC or other government organizations that are supposed to prevent outbreaks like this?"

Seth retorted, "Well, if they were supposed to stop this from happening, the world wouldn't be destroying itself right now, so I'd put my money on Dr. Hex. If it's this bad and the CDC or another organization allowed it to get this bad, it means they can't comprehend it. Just think about how strong he made us. He probably has other experiments, or he can create a solution to this problem."

Isis went on to ask, "How will we get there? We can't take a plane or anything, and driving would be risky. Furthermore, we still don't fully understand how the *blight* works."

"We don't have a choice because we can't get any more supplies due to the situation," Tomie said.

Akim agreed with Seth and said, "If it has gotten this bad, that probably means the government has collapsed. Dr. Hex is our best bet, but even if we make it back to New Jersey, how will we fix the world?"

Everyone began to contemplate other options as they sat in silence. Seth looked around and saw that no one was brave enough to take the risk.

He said, "Look, we don't really have a choice. Nobody must go, but we can't just sit here and wait. So, whatever you decide, I'll make it there on my own if necessary."

Everyone stared at Seth in disbelief.

Apollo was the first to speak up, "I can't let you go on your own."

They all concurred that they wouldn't let him go on this trip by himself. For several hours, they discussed their options and made plans to determine the best course of action. They agreed to take the cars, and in addition to packing all necessities, they remembered Dr. Hex's weapons, which they were all going to take for protection. When they had everything figured out, the first thing they did was load the car with supplies. Loading up on water bottles and non-perishable foods. They also packed supplies for their hygiene. After they finished packing, they agreed that they would leave first thing the next morning. They woke up at dawn and attempted to contact Dr. Hex. He still didn't answer which meant they had failed once more. As they made their way to the garage, they looked at a map to figure out which route would be the most efficient for them to take back to New Jersey. Once they decided on a route, their first destination was Tuba City, Arizona, which was two hundred and seventy miles away and nearly a five-hour drive.

Before officially leaving their haven, Ena said, "I think we need some form of leadership."

"I'd say Seth and Tomie should each lead one team. They both awakened their *blight* which is why it makes sense for them to lead, from there we can split the group fairly. Diana, Isis, and Apollo will stay with Seth," Ena said, Tomie will be accompanied by myself, Akira, and Akim. We're all balanced in skill and intelligence, so I know any of us can make good decisions if we need to."

Ena blushed in embarrassment and turned away, as she said, "Sorry I got carried away, if you guys have another idea, that's fine as well."

Seth responded, "No, no, that sounds great, I guess we couldn't have said it any better, we trust your judgment, it was well said. You guys follow me while I take the lead."

Tomie took the role of driving first with her group after everyone was satisfied with the plan. Finally, the scenery from the private area as the cars drove out, going from a nice, healthy grass-like area that was surrounded by trees to a dry, desert-like area, with the heat beginning to permeate the car. After traveling for about an hour, they arrived at the Hualapai airport, but there was little to be seen and no indication of any life. In the hopes of meeting someone who could explain what was happening, they prepared to drive to Seligman Airport. As they approached the airport thirty minutes later, they saw military tents, vans, and trucks in the distance.

Apollo's voice rose with excitement as he said, "Look, the military is here."

They drove up closer and got out of their cars to look for people. The first thing they noticed was the unbearable smell that became progressively worse as they walked towards the tents. As they got closer it became evident that the tents were damaged with scratches and bullet holes. The only people who were not bothered were Seth and Akim, everyone else held their hands and shirts over their noses.

"What the fuck is that smell," Diana exclaimed.

"Dead people and a lot of them, especially if it's this bad," Akim replied.

The moment he finished speaking, they peeked through a few tents to discover corpses that were rotting and covered in flies, maggots, and dried pools of blood. Isis clung to Diana because some of the victims had gunshot and scratch wounds. While the others made a slow retreat, Seth realized that the situation was likely worse than they anticipated.

He whispered loudly enough for everyone to hear him, "Get back to your cars, we need to get out of here right now! There's something off about this."

Seth pulls Akim to the side as everyone rushed back to their cars, "we need to look around to get a better idea of what's truly going on and take whatever supplies that we can. I don't think we came prepared for whatever this is."

Akim nodded and retrieved an axe from the trunk. He gave Seth a sword and said, "We should always keep some type of weapon on us too. We can never be too cautious."

Seth nodded in agreement. He warned the group, "Me and Akim will be back, do not follow us, but if anything happens don't leave the cars unarmed."

Seth and Akim returned to the military trucks and tents in search of supplies they could take. They discovered some battered military backpacks on dead soldiers; they removed the contents and stored the supplies. They took bandages, medicine, and other items that appeared useful. They searched the trucks and discovered an M4 rifle next to a deceased trooper. Akim examined it and put it with the stash. After some time, Seth and Akim circled back to each other.

Seth said, "This outbreak isn't like anything they showed on the TV."

Akim nodded and responded, "I've noticed, they must be trying to water down the situation for the survivors, this trip won't be easy."

Seth and Akim went back to the group so they could leave. When they returned to the cars, they noticed everyone was studying the map.

Seth asked, "What's the next move, no one is alive here seems as though it's worse than what we expected, this didn't just happen overnight."

Ena nodded, "Yea, this is bothersome. What's so bad that the military forces couldn't handle it. We were looking at the map and noticed there are schools, motels, and even stores in this area alongside a gas station. While traveling, we should always search what we can."

It wasn't a long drive, and they quickly passed a few stores that didn't seem worth the trouble of checking out. As they moved through the area, all they saw was trash being blown around and no one in sight. They continued to drive and came across several signs that directed survivors to a nearby school, not just one, but several scattered across the city. So, they pulled over to look at a map and discovered that the Seligman unified school district was just around the corner. They arrived at the location quickly and pulled up to find a school with red bricks and silver metal fences surrounding it.

Seth took the initiative, ordered everyone to remain in their vehicles and was about to enter the building alone. He peeked through the window, and there was still no sign of anyone. He turned his body slightly toward the cars and nodded. He went through one of the broken windows after looking at the building to get a better idea of what happened in the area. As he tiptoed around to avoid stepping on broken glass, he was sure to be quiet. He looked around and saw some outdated computers and filing cabinets. He observed adorable miniature artwork that children must have drawn on a wallboard, and pictures of students who may not even be alive anymore. He closed the door behind him and left the room. He looked down the hallway and noticed that one the room doors was broken. It was then that he realized he'd just left the main office. He began to walk slowly towards the broken door. When he entered the classroom, he saw several dead children who appeared to have been attacked, their faces beaten in and guts ripped out, along with a few bodies that appeared to be adults who were scratched with their limbs torn off and scattered across the room. *The blood was fresh, what the hell could have done this*? Seth noticed a bloody trail on the ground that led to a different classroom down the hallway. He could hear weak whimpers and the sound of bones breaking as he walked up to the room. When he entered the room, he saw two people with blood on their hands and mouths full of flesh. Seth took a few steps back, as he tried to process what he saw.

When those things turned around, their face was covered in scratches that appeared to have been self-inflicted, and their black veins could be seen through their skin. Seth ran further down the hallway to get away from the two things as they screamed in a disturbing manner and charged at him. As he approached the school's back door, he braced himself before he burst through it, and rolled on the dry cement floor. He quickly got up and drew his sword. When the first one began aimlessly swinging at him, Seth dodged it by chopping off one of the arms and finished with a thrust to the chest, afterwards he kicked it from the blade. Seth dropped his sword after the second one pounced on him and knocked him to the ground. He rolled back, kicked the thing off him, and got his sword. As Seth stood up, he realized the first one, he had attacked earlier wasn't dead. *I stabbed this thing through its heart. How is it still alive?* Seth was becoming agitated as they surrounded him growling and prepared to attack once more. He grabbed the hilt of his sword tightly and rushed through one, slicing it in half and drenching his clothes in blood. He then blitzed the final one, as he pierced its chest and pinned it to the ground. *There's no way I missed its heart this time.* Seth noticed that both were still alive as he waited for it to stop swinging. As he stood up, Seth ripped the blade from the thing's chest and drove it through its skull. After that, it eventually died. Seth walked over to the one he had cut in half and finished by running the blade through his head as well. After he stepped back and sheathed the sword, Seth then turned to face the creatures he just killed. *What are these things?* Seth was examining his surroundings when he realized that all the nearby structures appeared to be a part of the school. He could make out a middle-aged man waving at the entrance of one of the other buildings from a distance.

"Come over here, did you finally kill those

revenants? Come in quickly."

Seth jogged over to the building and went inside what seemed to be a gym, it was filled with sleeping bags, supplies, and people ranging from kids to adults.

"My name is Randy. Prior to the Collapse, I was one of the school's teachers. We all bunkered in the school buildings but had to retreat to this gym because some of our people got infected."

Randy explained, "We can clean out the main building and reassemble it thanks to you."

Seth thought to himself, *So that's what the infected look like? Has the Collapse only been going on for three months?*

Seth replied, "Well good luck to you and the others but I really have to get going."

Randy chuckled and said, 'Well, you should at least stay the night, it's not safe to travel that late, and if you need answers, feel free to ask the military men who arrived in this area after the airport nearby was taken over."

Seth informed Randy about the rest of his group and he was delighted to have them stay the night.

The group noticed Seth had blood stains all over his clothes as he jogged back, and they rushed out to check on him. They asked many questions and Seth told them to relax and follow him to the back. The group proceeded to the gym, and as they passed by the revenants that Seth had killed, he pointed to them, and stated, "those are the things that chased me through the main buildings, these people call them revenants."

After he returned to the gym with the others, Randy greeted them, and they all thanked him for letting them spend the night. With the sun setting and the temperature dropping, the group noticed two people heading outside to start a fire, so they all followed them outside and joined them around the fire. Their faces appeared as though they had given up hope and had nothing left to live for. Both people were dressed in filthy camo pants and green tucked-in shirts The women and man nodded at the group to acknowledge their presence and changed their gaze back to the fire.

Isis said, "I don't even know where to begin, but what happened to the world?"

The woman struggled to find the words to say, "Those things..." She began to cry and then asked, "How do you guys not know about the *Collapse*?" while she covered her face.

The man said, "Calm down, we have to stay strong for these people here," as he held her close to his chest. "Let me do the talking." He sat up and spoke to the group "I'm Vergil, and this woman is Amy. About a few months ago, the government issued orders for all branches of the military to protect civilians in all nations. Nobody had any idea what they were up against. People were killing each other, and then the dead began to rise. With no idea what was causing the problem and no idea where the Virus originated, the world began to fail state by state, country by country."

The group was speechless, so Akira asked, "So you're telling us the entire world is..."

"Yes, we lost connection to the rest of the world, so it's best to assume that everyone and anyone we don't see is dead," Vergil said, lowering his head. "It's always better to be prepared for the worst."

The group was at a loss for words, and despair was setting in. Seth asked, "How long ago was it when the airport fell?"

"Roughly a week ago, we had some injured survivors in the medical tents, and after a few minutes, it was a bloodbath," Vergil said while looking at Amy. "People were screaming and running, and my team did everything they could to save as many people as possible. But those revenants weren't dying. People who did not have their heads bashed in began to succumb to the infections. People became revenants, reducing our numbers and wiping out the entire camp, forcing me and Amy to flee and end up here."

Seth asked, "So how do you properly deal with revenants, I killed two, but we have a long trip ahead of us and we need all the information we can get."

Looking at the fire, Vergil said, "My best advice is to avoid them at all costs. If you must fight, avoid making noise or you will attract more revenants in the area, so stick to items like knives, machetes, axes, or whatever else you can find. When fighting them, destroy their brains, aiming for their hearts, or crippling them so they bleed out will not work. They can also infect you, so don't let them scratch or bite you, and don't let their blood get inside your wounds, mouth, eyes, or ears, or you'll turn. If at all possible, I strongly advise you to avoid confrontation."

Seth nodded, "Understood, we'll be on our way once the sun rises."

Vergil nodded and said, "I hope y'all have a safe trip, and thanks for clearing out the main building once again. We can give you some supplies before you guys leave. For now, try to get some rest."

After leaving Vergil and Amy, they returned to the gym to rest. Unlike the rest of them, Apollo and Akira had difficulty falling asleep. They couldn't stop thinking about their families and the endless possibilities of what could have happened to them, and nothing but hopelessness and terror washed over them. When they awoke, they began packing their belongings and loading the cars in preparation for the next location.

"Hey, don't forget to take some supplies, we can't repay you enough for taking care of those revenants," Vergil said as he approached them with a cart full of items. There were cases of water, gas, jerky, and canned food."

Seth only took the gas and water and responded, "We appreciate the hospitality, but we will be on the road. I won't take too much away from you because you have a community to look after here."

Vergil shook his hands and said, "I hope you all make it to where you're going. Good luck."

They said their goodbyes, loaded up, and started the drive to Ash Fork, Arizona, which was only minutes away. They arrived after a short drive and drove around the area, which didn't appear to have much to offer, so they parked to talk for a while before moving on.

Diana turned around to face them with the hot sun on their backs, and said, "Yeah, nothing here for us; we should keep moving. This location appears to be completely deserted."

Following a brief review of the route on the map, the group chose Tuba City as its next destination. It was about a two-hour drive, but Isis noticed that some of the group appeared to be depressed.

She said, "Hey guys we can do this. I can see the look in some of your eyes. I know you're probably worried about your families and the rest of the world, but we've already lost if we give up and don't even try. We're a team, and I'm confident that with all our abilities, we'll make it to New Jersey, and I'm confident that Dr. Hex will be able to help."

Diana smiled at how optimistic Isis was, with Akira asking. "But what if all of our families are gone? You remember what those soldiers told us, and you saw the look on their faces. What if there is nothing left to fight for?" Everyone was silent for a moment.

Somewhere in their hearts, they knew Akira wasn't wrong. With an imaginary goal in mind and no real answer, Tomie saw that Isis was trying to give the group hope.

"Even if that's the case, we have each other. We are family, we're all we got, and we are all we need."

Seth dragged Akira forward to his chest almost like a brotherly hug, "Yea, we got this, I do hope all of your families make it through this, but right now we have to focus on what we can control."

Akira nodded with the others ready to go. As soon as they were back in their vehicles, they drove away from Ash Fork. They stopped halfway through the long drive to Tuba City to eat and take a break.

Tuba City, Arizona

Seth devised a plan once they arrived in Tuba City. "It's still early, and this place has a few stores and buildings for us to loot, so instead of wasting the day and staying the night here. We'll head straight to Chinle, which is about a two-hour drive away. We'll stay for no more than two hours, take what we can, and get to the next city as soon as possible." Seth continued, "Remember, grab anything useful, avoid revenants at all costs, try not to make too much noise, and keep your weapons on you at all times from now on."

They moved to the back of the truck. Seth and Apollo waited for the others because Seth already had a sword and Apollo had an axe. Akira and Apollo decided to take the machetes as their first two choices for weapons. Ena was left to take the polearm after Diana took the last sword. When it came down to Tomie and Isis, the only weapons left were bows, arrows, knives, and guns.

Tomie looked at Isis and said, "I know you're not much of a fighter, so I'll take these knives, so you can use the bow and keep your distance."

Isis took the bow and looked at Diana and said, "Diana has been training me in her free time, so I'll do my best."

Seth and Tomie's group separated, both taking different routes to loot.

Isis suggested stopping by a healthcare facility after a while of trudging through the oppressive heat. She pointed it out. Before going to the entrance, they wandered through the building and assessed their surroundings. They arrived at the medical facility to find a few corpses lying on the floor and blood all over the place. As they moved through the door, Seth guided them while crouch-walking near the walls. When Seth entered the main office, he noticed that the computers were broken, there were papers all over the floor, and a map of the structure was hanging on the wall. He led them deeper into the building. They were on high alert because the halls were littered with bullet holes and blood. After reaching a door with a window slab, Seth peered in and noticed shelves of bottles, liquids, and other medical supplies. Seth attempted to open the locked door.

After looking around, he said, "I'm going to kick

down this door, and Isis will point out everything that's worth taking, while everyone packs it up as quickly as possible and get out of here."

Before Seth could act, Apollo stopped him and said, "We can't just be so hasty. We don't know what's in here."

Seth sighed and rolled his eyes, then replied, "It's now or never." We'll be in and out."

Then kicked the door which flew across the room. They all rushed in and took everything Isis pointed at from medicine containers, gauze, and first-aid supplies. They rushed out and ran through the halls, after they took whatever, they could carry. They saw a few crippled revenants struggling to make their way to them down one of the halls before reaching the exit. They briefly stopped when Isis ordered everyone to stop trying to get a better look at the crippled revenants. Once they got close enough, they could see that they had gouged out eyes, pale skin, and bullet holes, the group could hear their weak whimpers. After they were done examining the revenants Seth's group rushed out, making their way back to the cars. Tomie's group already had portable tanks of gas from a gas station, and with nothing in sight but the oppressive heat, they chose a different route back.

After a long walk without seeing anything, Akira pointed out a church with several dusty cars out front that appeared to be abandoned. He advised them, that they should search the church for supplies like food cans. Their stomachs began to turn as they drew nearer to the church, making them feel more uncomfortable. They could already hear a swarm of flies buzzing around behind the already cracked doors. The heat intensified an unpleasant odor that was permeating the area. Akira opened the door while intermittently throwing up from the smell of decomposed bodies. They witnessed flies and maggots devouring the corpses of babies, kids, and elderly people. Quotes such as "God has forsaken us," "this is the rapture," and "Hell on earth" were written in blood on the walls. They were horrified to see these withered revenants eating some of the corpses as they feasted in the shadows. While the others were struggling to consume the limbs of the dead, paying no attention to the group, one was biting into a baby's stomach and eating its guts out. Their minds were filled with despair as they shut the doors and left the building. When they had collected themselves, they headed directly for the cars, where Seth's group waited. As they prepared for the upcoming drive, they all looked over the supplies they had gathered. At this point, everyone was silent. They remained silent, and only reflected on what they saw so far. They were all already aware of their tasks, and if they couldn't save the world, who would?

Chapter V

HOME SWEET HOLE

Chile, Arizona

After a brief drive, the team eventually arrived in Chile, Arizona. As the sun began to set, they all got out of the car and walked around the seemingly deserted area. They looked around for nearby houses that appeared safe for them to spend the night in. They heard conversation and laughter in the distance. As they turned the corner, they came across a young boy who pushed a cart full of supplies. He was dressed in a filthy long-sleeved shirt with a vest over it. He walked alongside a girl who only had one arm. Her clothes were also filthy.

Isis called out to them and waved, "Hey!"

The young woman was alarmed.

"Henry, stay behind me!" she said as she stepped in front of the boy.

Seth stood in front of the group, and pleaded with her, "Hey, calm down, we're not going to hurt you. We are friendly."

The girl asked, "Where did all of you come from?"

"We're just passing through, trying to get to New Jersey," Seth replied. We were looking for somewhere to stay for the night, and we are going to leave in the morning."

The young lady was still asking questions, "Where did you get the weapons from and how are you traveling?"

Seth responded, "We have our own cars, and we had these weapons from the start. None of us want any problems."

The young lady looked at Henry, then looked at the group, and said, "You guys don't seem like you mean harm. You can come back with us for the night. My name is Hannah, and this is my little brother Henry."

With the tension starting to settle, they introduced themselves and followed her back to her house, which was not far from where they had parked their cars.

Diana questioned the young girl, "Why aren't there more people here? So far, we have only encountered one camp, where are the others?"

Hannah paused for a moment before responding, "I don't know, ever since the outbreak. Most of the people sought refuge in military camps set up at airports and major cities. However, with everyone gone, we had more supplies and less problems."

Diana asked, "What made you stay here with your brother?"

Hannah paused for a moment before responding, "Our parents died, and I didn't want to risk the trip and risk losing Henry. This is home, I could never leave it behind."

Diana looked down, and apologized. Hannah smiled as she approached the front door and said, "It's fine, and we made it." Once inside, Hannah directed them to the second floor and showed them where they could sleep. She returned and sat with the group after they settled in, while Seth went to the rooftop to get fresh air; he overheard Hannah laughing and talking with the group. Seth sat there and enjoyed the gentle breeze that blew against him. He gradually grew colder as the moon was fully illuminated.

"You know what you want," she said softly as the presence of a woman wrapped her arms around him.

It was the same woman's voice he'd heard before and although it was unsettling, her presence consoled him. Seth broke out in a cold sweat; his sclera was slowly devoured by darkness.

"What's the point of resisting yourself?" She continued, "I know what you desire, I can feel how much rage and hatred you have built up inside of you. Her voice echoed in his head as she spoke. "You and I both know what the real issue is." Slowly rising, Seth made his way back to the window. His eyes were as dark as night, and his iris shone purple like the nebulas in space.

"Slaughter them all."

Everyone sat around a few candles while they chatted with Hannah and snacked on chips. Isis asked, "So how did you lose your arm? I don't mean to bother you too much, but I'd like to look at it."

Hannah unraveled the raggedy bandages from her shoulder and said, "It's fine. It happened around the time of the *Collapse*. I sacrificed it to save Henry, I was bitten by one of those revenants, and I chopped it off with a machete."

Isis looked at the stub and said, "So you're telling me you can survive being infected by one of those things?"

Hannah replied with a chuckle, "Well, I didn't know, but I gave it a chance since my only other choice was to change into one of those things."

Tomie left the room to check on Seth when the room fell silent. Hannah then questioned the rest of the group about why they were traveling so far.

"You've barely scratched the surface of your power."

Seth raised his arm in front of him, guided by the presence of the woman. His arm began to bleed as his red blood turned darker than night. As his blood flowed to his palm some of it dripped from his arm. Now having a hand full of blood, the presence made him clench his fist, and the blood slowly formed into a pitch-black sword.

"Hey Seth, how are you holding up?" asked Tomie, who was coming through the window with her head hung low. After finally getting all the way through the window, Tomie noticed Seth didn't look so well, and looked down while he hid his face from her.

"I'm fine," he replied. "I'll be fine," Seth said as he raised his head, his eyes turning white as he made eye contact with Tomie.

Tomie, pressed for more answers, said, "You don't look so well, you're sweating and shaking. What's the matter?"

Seth took a seat and responded, "Ever since I had my *blight,* I've been getting these urges, I see and hear things that aren't there."

Tomie sat next to him, just listening as he continued, "I just want us to get to New Jersey safely, but something doesn't feel right." Tomie said, "I've heard voices too, but nothing to the point where I am seeing things. We must be having different reactions to the virus. When we get to Dr. Hex, he might be able to figure out what's wrong. Despite how chaotic the world is right now, we gotta travel to New Jersey if we hope to make any changes.

With annoyance in his voice, Seth retorted, "This world was messed up before the *Collapse*. There is no longer any government in charge, and there are no rules to abide by, which is the only difference now." As he spoke, Seth's hand formed into a fist. "But even with all of this, the world always seemed to be against people like us." Tomie just looked at Seth as he ranted, "I might be from a rich family and didn't have to go through the pain that people like us did in the past; but I've done my research, and I can't explain how much hate I have dwelling inside. Slavery, and people having the system against them just because of the color of their skin, other people being rejected or slaughtered for what they believed in; the conflict that humans have created never sat well with me. You got other people in the dark corners of the world, that are being killed, raped, abused, and others with miserable lives that didn't have a choice about whether they wanted to be here."

Tomie puts her hand over Seth's fist and replied, "When we make it to Dr. Hex, and get all of this situated, we can change the world as we see fit. A world where no one must struggle or suffer due to injustice. I'm not saying forget about the past but let's focus on what we can change. After everything is said and done, we can rebuild the world to become a better place."

Seth calmed down and looked at Tomie and replied, "You're right, we have to make all of this count."

Tomie smiled and said, "as long as we have each other anything is possible, let's go get some rest."

Seth nodded, and they both made their way back into the house.

While the others were taking a nap in the other room, Isis spoke to Hannah, "We have some supplies we can leave so you can take better care of your stub."

Hannah replied with a smile, "I really appreciate it. You must be the group's leader?"

"No," Isis replied, and laughed. "If I had to say, it's probably Seth, Ena and Tomie. We never decided on an official leader or anything, but they make most of the decisions and are the most powerful of all of us. Not that any of us are weak, I just can't bring myself to do what they can. I wasn't made for this world."

Hannah responded, "I see, that's how I was before the *Collapse*. I used to fear a lot of things and was never as strong as my father or mother. But something clicked one day, once I realized I had to fight and kill to protect what I have left." Hannah looked at her stub, and said, "I stopped holding back because I didn't want to lose home. Or whatever's left of it."

Isis had a dejected expression on her face as she pondered her earlier conversations with Diana. She said, "I see, sometimes you have to do things because there's no other choice."

To which Hannah replied, "Yea."

After a short conversation, they both decided to call it a night and get some sleep.

When the group awoke to Hannah screaming for help, they all rushed outside, not realizing there was an unpleasant odor was coming from somewhere in the house.

Hannah's arm was bleeding from what appeared to be a knife wound, and she begged, "Can you help look for Henry? I came across one of those revenants and we got separated. He shouldn't be too far away from a gas station."

Ena came up with a quick plan: "While Seth, Diana, and Apollo go check out the gas station and look around for any ideas as to where he might be, Isis and Akira stay here and tend to her wound. Me, Tomie, and Akim will search nearby."

In a rush, they all dispersed to go look for Henry. With no sign of any life anywhere and only the oppressive heat, Ena's group searched the area while they called out for Henry. They made the decision to explore further afield to see what they could discover.

Tomie slowed down for a bit, and said, "Guys, wait!" The group stopped to listen to Tomie. "We need to think of some other way or another possibility of what could have happened? What if he got attacked and turned, or is dead already?"

Akim replied, "Well we don't have any proof or any idea of where he could be, are we supposed to just leave him out here alone?"

Tomie shook her head and replied, "No, but we also have to be ready for the worst."

Ena agreed and replied, "that's true, but what do we do from here? None of this makes any sense, where and how could they get attacked if there wasn't anyone here?"

Tomie quickly responded, "Also if she got attacked by a revenant, wouldn't she have turned already?"

Isis hurried Hannah inside the house as everyone else searched for Henry.

Isis demanded, "Akira go to the cars and bring some of the medical supplies we need, gauze pills and alcohol." Right after he left, Isis brought Hanna to the couch, and said, "Everything's going to be ok, they'll find Henry."

When Isis turned her back, Hannah pulled a gun from her pocket and knocked her out, and said, "I'll be fine, but I can't say the same for you or any of your friends." Hannah locked the front door before using handcuffs she had pulled from a drawer in the living room to restrain Isis' hands behind her back. Then she dragged Isis downstairs to the basement and proceeded to lock her inside. Hannah heard Akira knock and smiled as she opened the door.

He said, "Hey, I got the bag of stuff here. Are you guys ok?"

"Yeah, everything's OK, come inside. Isis was waiting for you."

Akira hurried inside. He laid the bag on the ground and took the items out. "It smells like-" Akira gagged and recalled the smell of decayed bodies. Hannah used her gun to knock Akira out cold.

Due to the intense heat and the pressure of trying to find Henry, they stopped to try and collect their thoughts.

Seth said, looking off into the distance, "This doesn't make any sense, there is no one here."

"So how could they possibly have been

attacked?" Diana responded, "Who was she fighting to get all of those cuts?"

Seth shouted to the others, "Go get the others, I need to go check on Isis, and Akira!" he shouted in anger as he dashed back to the house at top speed.

Diana realized and said, "Hannah might be turning into a revenant. We've got to hurry and catch up with Seth!"

On his way back to the house, Seth noticed that the door had been left open and that a foul odor had taken over the atmosphere. He hurried into the house and the smell intensified. He heard noises coming from the basement and rushed downstairs. That was when he witnessed one of the most disturbing scenes in his life.

Hannah stood there with tears streaming down her face as she pointed a gun at Seth and screamed, "STAY THE FUCK BACK OR I'LL SHOOT YOU!"

The floor was covered in the remains of dead adults and children, and the wall was covered in blood and guts. Seth was drawn to the sounds of chains slapping, the slurping, and the crunching of bones in one of the dark corners. When he looked over, he saw a withered revenant feasting upon Henry. His guts spilled on top of other corpses, half of his body was torn apart, and his eyes were filled with terror and tears. Seth turned to Hannah and yelled, "WHAT DID YOU DO TO THEM!"

Hannah continued to point the gun at Seth, and said, "My father is getting weak and doesn't eat regular food anymore, so I had to do this. I gave him my arm because I wasn't strong enough to give him Henry at the time. But as the population got smaller and smaller, I began to run out of people to feed my father."

Seth clenched his fist as she talked, "Now that you all are here, I can feed him for a few more weeks."

Seth glared and waited a moment to get Hannah off her guard. "So, you're going to stand there and wait your turn! I WON'T ALLOW ANYONE TO TAKE MY HOME AWAY FROM ME!"

Diana and Apollo caught up with the other group as they hurried back.

Tomie, who was out of breath, said, "We gotta get back to the house." Everything about this situation seems strange. Where is Seth?"

Diana responded, "He ran back to the house and told us to bring you all back."

They increased their speed, attempting to return to the house as quickly as possible. Seth felt chills down his spine and felt that woman's presence again. Her voice echoed in his head, provoking him even more. His mind was consumed by rage, while his sclera was consumed in darkness. When Isis finally realized where she was, she immediately threw up because of the smell of all the rotting bodies. Hannah was distracted when Isis started to cry uncontrollably. Seth charged at Hannah, and she shot him twice right before he grabbed her by the neck.

Seth held her against the wall with one arm while he remained unaffected by the bullets. As Hannah grabbed his arm and swung her legs, she dropped her gun.

She said, "You can't be human... What are you?" before she passed out.

"I hope we aren't too late. Those were gunshots." Akim pointed out. "But we are almost there."

They all struggled to breathe once they got to the door, the foul odor of corpses filled the air.

Tomie and the others called out for them, "Isis, Akira! Where are you!"

Seth screamed from the basement, "Don't come downstairs!"

Seth then shot Henry to put an end to his suffering after shooting the revenant who was bound to the pipe. With no regard for Seth's words, Diana and the others sprinted downstairs. Once they arrived, they were shocked by what they saw. Henry was dead and half-eaten, and there were heaps of corpses on the ground. Seth turned around with a sad yet empty expression.

He said in a low tone, "I told you to not come down here, none of you had to see this."

The way he looked at them revealed that his *blight* was active, and they could see that he had been shot in the shoulder. Diana rushed to Isis as she wailed, while Akira was still unresponsive.

Diana tried to reassure Isis by saying, "It's okay now that we are all here. Let's get out of here."

Diana helped Isis up the stairs while Akim and Apollo carried Akira out of the basement. As Seth proceeded to drag Hannah by the hair up the steps, he disregarded her as her head hit every step along the way. They made their way outside to consider their options for handling her.

She said, "You took the last bit of home I had left," while she cried. As Seth held the gun to her head, she screamed, "GO FUCKING DIE!"

The group struggled to watch her in this state. Seth kicked her to the ground, cocked the gun and prepared to shoot her, but Isis stopped him.

"We can't just kill people, it's not right," Isis said as she gripped Seth's arm. "We can just leave her here."

The group looked away, and Tomie was the only one to side with Isis. She saw the look in Seth's eyes, and she didn't want him to lose himself.

Tomie said, "Isis is right, we can't just go around killing people; we don't have the right."

Diana got upset and replied, "What the hell? This bitch just tried to kill you, and then all of us."

Seth said, "Exactly, so I don't see what's so wrong with snipping out a few people if they try to kill us. Tell me this, would any of you here feed one of your siblings to a fucking revenant?"

Seth continued, "This piece of shit killed her own brother and nearly killed you and Akira, I'm not allowing her to live." They all turned away as he spoke. Isis's grip on Seth's arm loosened. "If you guys won't do the killing, I will. I'm not gonna let any of you die while I'm here." Seth looked at the group, with an emotionless expression said, "None of you here can stop me anyways. I'm the strongest here, and at this point, I'm the strongest man alive. So, if no one can make the right decision I will." Everyone remained silent, they knew he wasn't wrong.

Seth brought his attention back to Hannah, who threw a tantrum on the floor and begged to be killed, "I don't have anything else. Just kill me already, my home is gone…"

Seth glared at Hannah and grabbed her by the

back of her scalp. He said, "At least we're on the same page." Seth dragged her back to the house.

Hannah still sobbed and pleaded with Seth, "Just kill me already!"

While making his way downstairs, Seth bashed her face against the wall and threw her down the basement steps. Hannah cried on her knees on top of all the corpses she had led to that basement. Seth held the gun to her head, and the first shot splattered her brains against the wall, leaving her body twitching on the floor. He proceeded to waste all the ammo on her corpse. Afterward, he spit on her corpse and returned upstairs to join the rest of the group, who sat on the floor outside.

"Get the rest of the supplies out of this house before we leave," he demanded.

Without hesitation, they took everything they brought, and the supplies Hannah had. Seth went to get some matches and a tank of gas as they loaded the cars, then he headed back to the house. He soaked the floor in gasoline beginning on the top floor and moving down to the main floor and finally the basement.

After everything was soaked, he stood in the basement and looked at the horrific scene that Hannah left behind. Seth stared at Henry's charred remains, his guts protruded from his body, with his eyes open and dried streaks of tears remained on his face. The withered revenant, his father, laid beside him. Seth cast a glance over at Hannah, who had been reunited with her family in the sad hell hole she created.

"I will not allow any of them to die on my watch." Seth went outside and lit the matches before he tossed them into the house. He returned to the group once the house was completely engulfed in flames. Seth's *blight* had been deactivated by the time he returned to the others. He apologized, saying, "I'm sorry for snapping at you earlier, but I just can't let any of you die." As he prepared to see the next location, Seth pulled out the map. "This world has no rules," he continued, "so we must do everything we can to protect ourselves."

Akim agreed and said, "He's right, any decision we make can mean the difference between life and death. We have to be smart and do what is best for us." Isis didn't accept the fact that Seth had just killed someone.

She replied, "No, it's not okay. Killing someone or choosing violence is never the answer. We can't let the world change us from who we are."

Diana got irritated and said, "Isis please stop. Some people don't deserve your kindness, and if you keep going on with that mindset, you'll die in this world."

Seth looked around and realized the group was slowly breaking down. Seth said, "When we make it to the next stop, we can take a break. The next stop is Tsaile, Arizona. It's roughly an hour drive. We will find somewhere to settle today so we can relax. Then tomorrow we will continue. No one deserves to see what we all witnessed today."

Diana added, "We need to be ready because this is the world we live in today." Akira added to the conversation, "but Isis and Seth are both right, we can't just go through this without getting blood on our hands. We also can't allow ourselves to let this world numb us and change who we are."

The group took a moment of silence as the house crackled and burned in the distance... Seth looked at all of them, and said, "None of you are wrong, and none of us are right. I just want you to know that if anything comes between us, I will not hesitate or second-guess myself. We only have one goal: to make it to New Jersey alive."

When the silence took over the house had nearly burned down to the ground. They prepared to make the short drive to Tsaile, Arizona.

Chapter VI

NEW FACES

Tsaile, Arizona

It's been two months since the group found out about the *Collapse* and everyone sat in silence for the entire drive. Isis continued to cling to Diana and lean on her as the others ruminated about the past. The first thing Tomie's group noticed upon entering Tsaile was a church that made their stomach turn and reminded them of the terrible sight they just witnessed at the other church. The withered revenants feasting on corpses, blood smeared on the wall, and a smell that they could never forget. They arrived at a gas station and stopped to plan their next move. Ena pointed at the map and stated,

"There are a few schools nearby. There might be supplies that we can take, and then we buckle down for the day."

Everyone agreed while Akim added, "We need to be armed properly from now on. I've been thinking about how we've been running around with these weapons; we need to keep a low profile from the revenants, and we need to be prepared for humans. We can't allow ourselves to be vulnerable again."

Seth added, "I agree, but who here has knowledge on guns?"

Seth, Akim, and Ena were the only ones to raise their hands. Akim said, "From now on, the ones who know how to shoot should always have one. Throughout this trip, we will train the rest of you."

They prepared to split up after loading their firearms. Ena gave them the strategy and directed Seth's group to go to the college. While Tomie's team investigated the elementary school. They were going to spend the night at whichever school appeared to be the safest.

They split from the gas station, leaving the cars behind. Tomie noticed Akira's mood and asked him, "You still thinking about the Hannah situation?"

Akira looked at Tomie and then kept looking forward as he spoke, "Yea, me and Isis almost died. If it weren't for Seth, we probably wouldn't even be here right now."

Tomie took a moment to respond, trying to find the right words to say. She replied, "Don't think about what could've happened. We are all here and alive. We just need to be more careful about the people we come across-"

Akira interrupted her; "No. That's not the point; I'm weak. I let a bitch with one arm get the best of me. Seth had to get blood on his hands for us." Akira clenched his fist, "I'm not strong like you, Seth, Ena, or Diana. If that's not bad enough, I can't even activate my *blight* if I needed to do so."

Tomie replied, "We are here as a team. Don't worry about your individual strength. We will continue to do everything as a team and build on that. Hannah was a snake. Who would've expected someone to do something so cruel."

Akira looked at his hands, and replied, "True. But part of me also thought that if I was strong enough, maybe we wouldn't have to kill people. I never thought any of us would have to cross that line. Taking someone's life can't be that easy."

Tomie agreed, "True, but that wasn't a normal situation. Seth made the call, even though half of us weren't comfortable with the outcome. We knew he wasn't wrong."

Body parts were strewn about the front and other areas of the octagon-shaped college as Seth's group neared the entrance. Everyone pulled out their weapons on high alert. Apollo noticed some of the bodies had fresh blood and asked, "Do you think other people could be holding off inside?"

Diana responded, "At this point, it could be people or revenants. Just stay on guard."

They entered the building, each watching the others back, with Isis closer to the center. After they moved through some of the hallways, they heard screaming. The group stopped for a moment, and Seth whispered, "Those must be revenants, and it sounds like a lot of them. We must get out of here before we get swarmed." Seth collapsed to the ground and screamed in agony, "Please get out of my head!" As soon as he finished his sentence, they could hear revenants closing in as they screeched and ran toward the group. Apollo helped Seth get up by grabbing his arm.

Apollo demanded, "Come on. Get up, we gotta go!" The group was running, trying to escape the revenants, with Seth trailing behind. Diana finally reached a door that appeared to be locked.

"The doors are locked!"

As a group of revenants drew near, Diana pushed Isis back and prepared to fight them. The revenants were riled up and more alert than usual. A revenant who was clinging to Seth's leg had its arm severed by Apollo. That gave Seth enough time to shoot a few of the revenants. Another revenant jumped on top of Seth, clawing at him. Diana kicked it in the face, giving Seth time to unsheathe his sword. Seth killed one of the revenants by thrusting his blade through their skull. Another revenant pounced on Seth, and both grabbed and bit his arm. Seth screamed in pain, hitting the revenant off. Isis shot the revenant that bit Seth with her bow and arrow. Seth glanced at his arm before turning to face the final three revenants, not realizing that his eyes had turned back to orange.

Seth said, "Get behind me, I've been bitten!" He then pushed Apollo aside and rammed his sword through the head of a revenant. *I feel weaker already. Am I turning...?* He struggled to get the blade out of the revenant's skull. Seth finally freed his sword by kicking the revenant corpse. He then kicked one of the revenants to the ground before snatching the second by the neck with all his might. Seth chopped off its head after he rushed it to the wall. Eventually, Seth dropped his sword and ran to the final one. He pushed it to the ground and started to repeatedly punch its head, while the rest of the group stood guard, and kept an eye on Seth. He eventually came to a stop, sat on the ground next to the dead revenants, his knuckles bloodied and bruised. He turned to face his friends. He said in a low tone, "This is the end of the line for me. I guess this is how it ends." Seth picked up his gun and chuckled when he realized he only had one bullet left *how poetic.*

Seth said, "I can't risk the safety of the group. You guys go on without me, and let the others know what happened."

Isis stopped Seth before he put the gun to his head. Diana and Apollo kneeled next to Seth, and they all realized his eyes weren't purple anymore. Isis said in a sad tone, "There has to be something that we can do."

The group heard footsteps around the corner and noticed a young man.

He said, "Follow me, hurry!"

They entered what appeared to be the cafeteria after following the man down the hallway. They noticed two other survivors. One of them was attempting to assist the other, who appeared to be injured and lying on the ground.

Seth asked, "What happened here?" The young man who wore thick layers of raggedy clothes, explained.

"We've been holding out in this city for a while. This college, and an elementary school around the corner, have been our homes ever since the *Collapse*. But just a few moments before you arrived, all those runners you killed were from our group. I don't know what happened, but one became two, and two became four. They all started going crazy and killing each other. We are the only ones that made it. So, we will be heading to the elementary school since that seems to be the safest bet." Seth was at peace knowing that Tomie's group was safe.

Seth said, "Well, as you can see. I got attacked. I won't be able to go on any further."

The man asked, "Wait if you got attacked, how are you still sane? In most cases, from what we've seen, people start going crazy within seconds to a few minutes, killing everything in sight, turning into runners."

Seth looked at his group. The injured person then started to scream and claw at the person who was watching over them. The group shifted their attention to the girl. Everyone on guard was keeping their distance when Diana asked, "What happened? How did she turn? Was she injured by a revenant?" The guy slowly backed up and fell to the ground, tearing up.

He cried out, "N-no, she was injured from something else. How did she turn." The new revenant was focused on them, charging at the group. Seth stood his ground in the front. When he reached for his sword, Isis shot it down with an arrow before it could get any closer. Isis took the time to wrap up Seth's arm as the man sobbed over the death of his group. Seth looked at his friends and said, "This may be the end for me, I don't want to be seen like this in my final moments. Nor do I want to waste any more resources. I-"

Diana was irritated and said, "Shut up already, you aren't dying on us, and we aren't leaving you behind. Did you forget what he said? You would have already turned into one of those things. But I'm pretty sure we are all thinking the same thing."

Isis smiled and added, "Yeah, due to you having the *blight* activated, it must have prevented you from turning." Isis turned to Diana and said, "See Diana, I told you this *blight* had potential for more."

Apollo added on, "But he no longer has the *blight*, by the look in his eyes. The real question is whether it must be activated or if anyone with the *blight* like us and Dr. Hex has immunity."

Seth laughed and said, "But isn't this great? That means we are on the right path. We were right. Dr. Hex is the key. So, our objective is clear now. We gotta' make it to the others and let them know. Hopefully they will have better luck than us."

Tomie's group was already inside the elementary school. Andrew, the leader there, allowed them to stay, seeing as they met no harm and were just looking for a refuge, as they waited for Seth's group to arrive. After a while, a guard came to escort them to the nurse's room.

The guard said, "Our group at the college was completely wiped out. Only one of our guys returned."

Ena asked, "What about our people? What happened to them?" Kevin took a moment before responding, "They all made it back, but I got word that one of them was bitten."

They made it to the nurse's room, where they saw Seth's group alongside the last survivor, explaining what happened to Andrew. Andrew rubbed Colby's shoulder, and said, "Colby, I need you to explain what happened at the college."

Colby, tried to get himself together and said, "It all happened so fast, one-person turning led to another, and it spread like a wildfire. At first it was me and a few others trapped in a room. Honestly, I didn't think we were gonna' make it. But after some time, we heard other people out there fighting and shooting, and if it weren't for their group, I'd be dead with everyone else. They killed all those runners. Sadly, this guy right here was bitten in return."

Seth unraveled his arm to show them the injury, while Tomie's group was in disbelief. Andrew walked over to Seth and inspected his arm.

He asked, "So how is he not turning, showing no symptoms?"

Seth wrapped his arm back up and looked at his group, he then said, "I guess it's not really a secret anymore. We are all part of a project testing out this human enhancement called the *blight*. Long story short, it increases all your physical capabilities. Now, luckily for me, we learned that it gives me immunity to these revenants."

Andrew chuckled a bit, not knowing how to react. He replied, "If it weren't for you standing in front of me right now, I wouldn't believe you. But there is no way it can be a joke if you're still standing here and are able to function."

Seth smiled and responded, "I wouldn't either, but this is the reality of our situation. Our goal is to make it to New Jersey so we can fix all of this."

Colby wiped his face and stated, "I'm going with their group." Everyone was stunned by his statement.

Seth replied, "We can't offer any protection, and don't have much space in the cars."

Colby stood up and clenched his fist. He said, "I never wanted protection; I want a way to fix all of this. You guys seem to have an objective instead of sitting on your asses all day playing daycare."

Andrew stood in front of Colby demanding, "WATCH YOUR MOUTH BOY, you already know we can't afford to do anything with all these younger ones and kids around. Our best bet is to stay put until someone-"

Colby punched Andrew before he got to finish his sentence, making him fall to the floor shouting, "YOU SAY THE SAME SHIT, OVER AND OVER AGAIN. WE CAN'T KEEP WAITING; MOST MY FRIENDS ARE DEAD. EVERYONE THAT WAS IN THAT COLLEGE DIED LISTENING TO YOUR ORDER TO WAIT UNTIL HELPED ARRIVE BUT IT NEVER WILL." Colby turned to the group and stated, "I'm coming with you guys, I won't stay here any longer holding on to false hope. I'll grab my own ride and a few other people I know who would like to join."

The group looked around at each other and shrugged; they didn't know how to react.

Andrew got up and rubbed his face and said, "I apologize for not being the leader that you need. If this is your calling, I won't stop you." Andrew looked at the group and said, "I know this may be asking much, and a promise won't guarantee anything, but on this journey, can you watch out for my people as if they were yours."

Ena spoke for the group, "I assure you; we will do our best and take care of them as if they were family." Andrew left while the group was escorted back to their room.

While they were sitting in a circle and eating, they discussed what the next plans were.

Akim said, "So are we really going to allow them

to tag along? It's already a risky trip. No one here is promised to make it to New Jersey."

Diana, who was playing with her food replied, "doesn't seem like he means any harm. If he keeps up, can we really turn him away, besides it's the end of the world. What's the worst that can happen?"

Apollo added, "The more people we have the better right? Imagine us with our own army. Making it to New Jersey won't be so stressful."

Ena finished her bowl of food and replied, "It's not that simple sadly. The concept of having more people is nice, but we also need to keep in mind our resources. The higher the headcount, the faster we burn through supplies. If we were building a base while gathering and growing supplies that would be a different story. But we are trying to get to New Jersey while cutting stops to a bare minimum. Even if we take time and scout for supplies, they will go faster than we gather them. All I'm trying to say is that we need to be mindful."

Tomie agreed with Ena and said, "True but some gains come with losses. If we acquire more people, they are bound to have knowledge and different skill sets which could be helpful in the long run. We just need to make sure that if it comes down to it, we have the good people on our side."

Seth butted into the conversation, "the only thing that matters is getting to New Jersey. No one was right or wrong in this conversation. The simple goal is that we make it to New Jersey asap. If they don't pose a threat and can keep up, I don't see the problem with them joining. We all saw how passionate he was about leaving and making a change. It would be nice to have people with the same common goal. To save the world, we should get some rest. By tomorrow, we will be in New Mexico. Ena is right about the supplies, which means we will have to put in more work, but that is something we will have to prepare for."

After they cleaned up and got ready to sleep, they all took their respective parts of the room and laid down. Moments after the lights went out, most of the group was sleeping. Isis tossed and turned, trying to force herself to wake up. Finally, she sat up in a rush, and reached out as if she was trying to grab someone's hand, only to realize there was nothing but darkness in front of her. She was sweating and breathing hard as she adjusted her eyes to the moonlight. She could see that Akira was wide awake and noticed he was crying. Akira wiped his face and looked over at Isis.

He began to speak with a weak tone, "I can't sleep, I can't eat, and I can see you struggling also." Akira covered his face as he cried out, "I couldn't protect you when your life was on the line. I couldn't even fight for myself." I

sis gripped her shoulders tightly as she brought her knees up to her chest... She replied, "It's not your fault. No one knew until it was already too late. Even then, I was naive to let my guard down like that, and if it came down to it. I wouldn't be able to protect myself either, so that isn't a weight anyone else should have to carry." The two didn't realize Seth woke up and laid there listening to the rest of their conversation.

Akira wiped his eyes and replied, "I'll just become stronger. How can we save the world if we can't save each other? We need to be able to fight for the weak, we need people who are going to fight for a change. Making our way to New Jersey is a team effort. So, we are here to fight and protect each other, alongside anyone else we can. The goal is to save the world."

After some time, Akira and Isis tried to get some rest but every time Isis closed her eyes, she could only remember that basement filled with corpses.

The group woke up the next morning to see Colby, (a Caucasian guy who couldn't be any taller than 6-foot, brown hair, and eyes, fit, wearing a thick layer of clothes.) They entered the room with supplies for him but instead found him all packed to go, he said, "I have my own vehicle and two of my people are ready to go. I've briefed them on the situation, and we are fully prepared. We all share the same goal of changing the world for the better, and we are all tired of wasting time here. When you guys are ready, we will meet in the front and leave from there."

Seth looked at the others impressed. Seth replied, "Right, we will be out in a few. We will discuss the next destination and plans before we leave."

Once they made it to the entrance, they saw Andrew talking to Colby. Andrew spoke, "You know, I've been thinking about what you said the other day. You're right, I can't sit here and allow more people to keep dying. So, while you guys are out on your missions, we will be trying to take over more land and expand the group. We are going to be making plans for expansion, starting with hitting the military bases they have nearby, getting supplies, recruiting people, and taking over land little by little." Andrew smiled and added, "so when you guys accomplish your goal, there will be something to come back to."

Everyone said their goodbyes, while Seth and Akim went to get the cars. Colby hugged Andrew and said, "We will do our best, once we get back, I'll tell you about everything."

Andrew patted Colby on the back, "I know you will. We also have some supplies to give you all before leaving; it will get hard out there but just remember you all have each other."

When Andrew said that it made them think of Dr. Hex. By the time they finished talking, Seth and Akim arrived with the cars, and Colby introduced the group to the other.

"This is Bellatrix. (an Indian woman, 5'6, athletic, straight black hair to her back, who wore thick, ragged clothes) and Brian (a Caucasian guy, 5'10, average build, with short black hair, and blue eyes, who also wore the same thick-ragged long-sleeved shirt that covered his thermal). "I've known these two since I was a kid, and we are all ready."

Bellatrix chimed in, "We are ready for all of it, the risk, and rewards. We all know this won't be easy, and we've heard about this *blight*." Bellatrix looked at Tomie's eyes and said, "We understand we are not equal in strength, but together I know we can make a difference."

Ena replied, "You're right, as long as we do this together as a team, we should be able to do everything, no one here will treat you like a liability. We all have the same goal." After they got over the small talk, they briefed them on the next plan and got ready to leave.

Once they got on the road and passed through

Wheatfields, they decided to pull over at Wheatfields Lakeside. While they admired the view of the lake, they all snatched up something light to eat. Brian reminisced, "When I was younger, my father took me here on the weekends to go fishing. I've always enjoyed spending time with my old man back then. Having the nice warm sun on your back, learning how to tie knots.... still a beautiful sight. But now it just seems so lifeless and gray."

Apollo asked, "what happened to your father?"

Brian explained, "He died before I graduated from high school from a cancer we never knew about. That left just me and my mother, who committed suicide a few days before the *Collapse*. Part of me was angry at the world for a while, but seeing how everything is turning out. I'm just happy they didn't die from being eaten alive by one of these monsters." Colby patted Brian on the shoulder. With the conversation feeling a bit heavy, they sat in silence and looked back at the lake. As they started to walk back to the cars Seth stopped Brian and said, "You're a strong person. A lot of people wouldn't have made it this far considering the things you've been through. I just want you to know we appreciate you joining us on this long trip."

Brian nodded and shook his hand, "Of course, I still want to live on and someday raise a kid the way my father did with me." Back on the road now, with a long drive ahead of them and nothing much in sight, some of the passengers fell asleep as they drove in between the border of New Mexico and Arizona. After some time, they finally made it to Gallup, New Mexico.

Gallup, New Mexico

With more people meant more supply runs, they had to find somewhere to park before they continued. The sleeping ones woke up to the sound of the others getting out of the cars and talking. They huddled around the vehicles and stretched as they looked around. They noticed that there were more buildings and stores around than houses. Colby asked, "So what's the game plan, will we scavenge here and find somewhere to stay for the day or?"

Ena spoke up for the group, "Since we have a bigger group, we should be able to cover more ground easily, it's still early so if we give ourselves some sort of time limit, we can loot whatever stores we can. Continue to the next location and find somewhere to settle over there before it gets too dark. We were splitting into groups of two, but now since there are eleven of us, we can split into three different groups and have a two-man group on the side, with our most capable people."

Bellatrix interrupted, "What about the cars? We need to protect whatever we already have. There will be people out there that we must be mindful of."

Apollo added, "We haven't really encountered too many people on the road where we had to defend the cars."

Seth stopped Apollo and said, "The idea is safety not about what we never encountered. She's right, No one has direct contact with your phone, but we use passwords for a reason."

Ena nodded, "True, so let's split into three teams. Group one will be Seth, Apollo, and Brian. Group two, Diana, Akim, and Colby. The last team will be me, Akira, and Bellatrix."

Bellatrix added, "you guys can just call me Bella since we are a team now."

Bella's energy made the group smile, as she seemed so happy to be around... Ena looked at Isis and Tomie, "Since you still have your *blight*, and no one can physically stop you. You will stay near the cars. While Isis, will go to the top of one of the buildings and keep an eye out with her bow. Even if you don't want to kill anyone, you can at least warn Tomie about anything out of the ordinary."

Bella was excited and said, "Wow this is gonna' be great! Ena you're so cool."

Seth looked up into the sky and said, "We have about two hours to make it back here so don't stray off too far."

While the group was breaking off in different directions, Diana checked in with Isis to make sure she would be ok. Diana said, "Remember what we talked about and promise to protect yourself before trying to play nice girl."

Isis hugged her and agreed before she left. Isis left to get into position as she wished Tomie good luck. Wandering past a few buildings she tried to see which one would be the easiest to get up to the top. She tried to open a few store doors that seemed to be locked or barricaded. She switched her plan and aimed for a different approach. She walked into the back alley and saw a fire escape that reached the rooftop. She rushed over and climbed the ladder. In no time she made it to the rooftop.

She smiled and waved, as she tried to get Tomie's attention, "Made it!" She called out. Tomie stopped eating her snack to smile and wave back.

Seth, Apollo, and Brian from group one already had a bag half-filled with goods and canned foods that they had discovered while passing by a dollar general and convenience store. Brian pointed out a gas station in the distance and said, "We got another hit to make." As they hurried over, they surveyed the building and noticed a few dead bodies but nothing of value to take. To determine what was still in the tanks, Apollo grabbed a few of the gas canisters while Seth continued to walk away to see what was still in the distance. He saw a hospital off in the distance once his vision was sharp. He looked at his injury and took a deep breath. He then continued to enjoy the sun on his skin as he gazed up at the sky and thought to himself. *I won't be strong enough to protect the others without my blight. However, it could have been worse; I could be dead right now.* He headed back to the others, informing them about the hospital he saw in the distance.

Seth said, "Our last stop can be the hospital, then we can start heading back with what we have." The other two agreed. They finished up at the gas station and made their way toward the hospital.

The search by group two, Diana, Akim, and Colby, was successful. They were in a grocery store, where they already loaded a cart with supplies and canned food that they could use on the journey. Diana, realized they were reaching their limit and said, "alright one more sweep to find anything else that looks useful, then we will head back." The others nodded and continued to look for what else they could find together while Diana wondered by herself.

After Colby was sure he and Akim were out of range of Dianna, he asked, "Is she single? She is fine as hell, with that Russian accent, tall and I know she is probably a top. Do you think I'm her type?"

Akim chuckled and said, "Wipe the drool from your face. Maybe we can find a collar and a leash with some doggy treats the way she got you."

Colby playful shoved Akim while they both laughed, Diana heard them in the distance and said to herself, "What could possibly be so funny? Boys are always easily entertained," as she looked at a shelf full of women's care products.

Group three, Ena, Akira and Bella already had a decent number of supplies. Before returning to their vehicles, they decided to look around one more store. They moved in the direction of the Walgreens that they could see in the distance. Bella was curious, "So when you guys make it to New Jersey, what is the plan to save the world?"

Ena responded to the unexpected question, "The scientist that gave us this thing he calls *blight,* will be located there. We believe that he should be able to fix all of this, and once that is settled, we will have to rebuild the new world.

The fact that Seth isn't one of those things, proves that the Blight can be the answer to solving all of this."

Bella was filled with energy and replied, "you know one of these days we will be in a documentary, or a movie after we pull this off." Her enthusiastic energy made the other two laugh and smile.

Ena said, "This will be a long trip, but if we pull this off, our lives can finally go back to normal."

Akira corrected her, "When we pull this off. We don't have a choice but to do so. We can't stop no matter what happens, and we won't stop until we make it to New Jersey." They arrived at the store, and searched the area to make sure it was safe to scavenge.

Ena got back to the others and said, "Nothing but a few dead bodies. We can grab what we can and get back to the others." As they dispersed, they came across several damaged goods, broken supplies, and corpses inside the store; but they continued to take what they needed.

Group one arrived at the hospital. They circled the building in search of the entrance. While doing so, they observed blood splatter, bullet holes, and boarded-up areas in some places. After taking a few steps back, Apollo turned to face the other two.

He said, "I don't think we should go in there." Seth looked at Apollo and turned back to the hospital.

Seth replied, "I'll do it myself. I wasn't planning on leading you two in there anyway. You guys wait out here, give me twenty minutes and I will be out."

Brian was perplexed by the idea and said, "No you can't go in there alone. This place is already giving me a bad feeling. I don't think it's safe or a good idea to even waste time here."

Seth started to get irritated with his team. He said, "It's not safe anywhere, so when did that matter? We don't have Isis here to know exactly what to grab. We never know when we will need something or when we will ever run out of supplies. So, like I said, give me twenty minutes and I will be back. I'll grab what I can." Apollo and Brian looked at each other, not knowing how to stop him. While Seth walked into the building, Apollo and Brian leaned on two of the abandoned cars that were nearby in the parking lot waited for Seth.

With his sword drawn and on guard, Seth moved cautiously through the structure. As he moved through the deteriorating hospital, the interior was covered with blood and bullet holes, wires were sticking out of the ceiling, and the lights flickered as they struggled to stay on. As Seth moved further down the hallway, he noticed a few rooms that were still intact. He began to regret not listening to the others and felt compelled to return with useful items for the group. As he got closer to one of the rooms, he looked through the glass window and noticed supply cabinets. The door wasn't locked, so he was able to open it. At once he started to store various pill bottles, bandages, and anything else that appeared to be useful. As soon as he left the room, he noticed something moving erratically and aimlessly down the hallway. Seth was unable to return the way he had come. He took a brief pause and considered finding another exit. Seth realized what it was. A revenant. It began to scream and bang its head against a wall, which caused hordes of revenants to burst through the doors and down the hallway. From the sounds of it, more were heard on the floors below and above. Apollo and Brian heard the noises coming from inside the building.

Brian said, "What the hell was that scream? That couldn't be Seth." Seth put the sword away and hurried past empty beds and cabinets to the stairwell in front of him. He ran up a few flights of steps, while some already started tracing him. Revenants poured out of the doors as he attempted to enter one, so he ran up more stairs. When he reached the top floor, he ran across the floor, dodging more stray desks and beds and tripping over stray papers as the revenants closed in. Seth noticed there was nowhere else to go other than out the window. He quickly looked outside to determine whether he could leap to the rooftop, which appeared to be about two floors away. Then he looked back at the horde of revenants.

He stepped back a bit before charging through the window, shoulder first, and rolling onto the rooftop, breaking his arm. He looked up to see the revenants raining out of the sky. When Seth stood up to try to distance himself, so many of them crashed onto the rooftop forcing it to collapse. Brian and Apollo were watching all the chaos that was going on.

Brian said, "What the hell, are all those revenants!? We gotta help him somehow."

Apollo was in complete shock and said, "But how? He doesn't have his Blight and even with the others we can't fight all of those." Seth was on his back, and he struggled to get up out of all the rubble. He screamed in pain, and realized there was a thin metal rod stuck in his shoulder pinning him to the ground, and he was tangled in a bunch of wires. Some of the revenants that followed him were now crippled and crawling, as they tried to get to him. Seth, attempted to force himself up and realized there were more revenants in the room he fell into. He screamed, "Fuck, Fuck, Fuck, I DON'T WANNA DIE, I DON'T WANNA DIE, I CAN'T DIE HERE!"

That same eerie yet comforting presence of a woman whispered into his ear, "So allow me to help you, stop resisting me." Seth's pupils shrank, with his sclera faded into complete darkness and his iris shone like the cosmos. Brian and Apollo heard a sound like a crash near the area where they last saw Seth, Apollo said, "We've gotta get back to the others now and get help!"

They rushed back to where they left the cars. Seth stood up. He ripped the rod out of his shoulder and black blood flow down his arm into his hand. His blood formed into a pitch-black sword.

All Seth heard was her voice echo in his head, "kill them all." He rushed at the revenants, and laughed while he ripped through them with ease. He didn't kill them properly. Instead, he chopped off limbs and cut the revenant heads off, as he became drenched in blood. Seth grabbed one by its face, and completely crushed its skull with his bare hand. A revenant leaped at Seth, and he grabbed it by the neck and ran it through a wall, as he tore its head off.

In his head her voice echoed, "Doesn't this feel great! aren't you having fun?"

The whole horde was still being slaughtered, walls were being broken down, and Seth was wreaking havoc as his heart raced. By the time Apollo and Brian made it back, everyone was already there waiting and talking. Brian rushed to the car, "get in and follow us, hurry, Seth needs help, he is surrounded by revenants, we need to go now!" They all rushed into the cars and followed Brian to the hospital. Seth succumbed to the power he regained as he slaughtered all the revenants that came through the building's floors and walls. Seth was covered in blood, as he laughed, and slayed every revenant in sight.

He continued to hear the woman's soft voice as she said, "See what happens when you stop resisting me, I can give you all the power you need."

After half of the building was destroyed, with only crawlers left. Seth couldn't control himself; he was only able to spectate his body. It was like being on autopilot he looked for more to kill, as he stomped on the crawlers and the corpses of what remained.

Seth realized, he was stuck in his head as he heard that woman's voice whisper in his ear, "This is what you want right, this is the beauty of annihilation." Seth sat down and was surrounded by darkness, as he held his head. He responded, "No, I just wanted to live." He watched his body as though he was watching T.V. At this point it was in control by something else.

The woman's presence hugged him from behind,

"Just sleep, let me handle everything from here on out."

Seth's blinks grew longer as he felt more at ease. His body was seen leaving the demolished structure as he wandered. "SETH, SETH" the group rushed out the car, trying to get his attention. His body turned towards the group, as he gripped his Blight weapon.

He could still feel the woman's presence as she whispered in his ear, "Let me handle everything from now on, I will fulfill whatever you desire." Seth's eyes widened after seeing the group, "No leave them out of this." The woman's presence tried to cover Seth's eyes, "Shhhh, you don't need them, you're the strongest."

Seth saw Tomie before everything went completely dark, "NO GET OUT OF MY HEAD!"

The surrounding darkness turned back into reality. He slowly gave in to exhaustion and fell to the ground. Seth had passed out and could not understand the muffled screams and voices of his friends. "Seth get-up! We gotta go! We can't stay here!"

He heard a man's voice, "Help him up! Get him in the car!"

Revenants and other infected will be drawn to the area because of all the destruction. They rushed Seth into one of the vehicles to get away.

Chapter VII

HERO // SANTA ROSA

Grants, New Mexico

Seth awoke abruptly out of his sleep in a cold sweat as he reached around the ground for his sword, "Stay away from my friends!"

Isis tried to help him calm down, "Relax, everything is ok, we are all safe."

Seth took a moment, looked around and noticed he was no longer covered in blood. Now he felt the heat of the campfire that everyone sat around, as they looked at Seth with concern. "W-where are we?" he asked softly as ran his hands through his hair and held his head, "My head is killing me, what happened."

Ena told him. "You were out for almost two hours. After we left, we made it to Grants, New Mexico as planned. We found you trying to leave that hospital, covered in blood, and the building was almost destroyed. Then you just collapsed, what do you remember?"

Seth looked around, "I went inside for supplies,

then got surrounded and swarmed by a horde of revenants, but I acquired my Blight again, for some time I wasn't in control of myself until I saw you guys. I just remember hearing this woman's voice."

Isis tried to give Seth some comfort, "Well the supplies you dragged out are useful for the most part, some were damaged due to obvious reasons, but at least it was worth it-"

Brian cut Isis off, "No we told him not to go in there, me and Apollo had a bad feeling about that place. What made you take a risk we didn't need too."

Seth, saw how worried everyone looked and said, "I did it for you all, just because we have supplies doesn't mean we will always have them. I felt as though it was best for the group, so I did it by myself. I didn't mean to cause any trouble; I just wanted to make sure everyone here does-"

Tomie cut him off, "No, cut it out. We are a team. It's a reason why we plan and do things together. No one here is alone, and no one here must go through this alone. We have each other for a reason, so next time numbers rule."

Seth checked his shoulder and realized the injury from the rod was healed already, "Understood, sounds fair enough."

Everyone still looked at Seth in silence, Isis was

the first to speak up, "Seth... you had everyone worried, we know that you're strong, but anything can happen, and we can't afford to lose each other."

Diana chimed in, "She's right, but we are stronger in numbers so keep that in mind when you decide to do something alone. No one here wants to lose you."

Seth, saw that everyone was concerned, "I truly do apologize." He took a long pause before he said, "I'll listen more, I'll do better. So, what's the plan now?"

Ena filled Seth in, "We will stay here for the night, we already cleared out one of the nearby houses. Ena paused for a bit, "But what voice did you hear and what did it say to you?"

Seth looked away before he responded. He thought about how he almost slaughtered his friend. "These voices I've been hearing for a while... I thought it was nothing to be concerned about, but after some time it got worse. When I started to struggle inside the hospital, she reached out to me. That's how I reactivated my *blight*, but I wasn't in complete control. It felt like I was slowly losing myself. But when you guys came, I came back."

The group was at a loss of words for a moment, Seth continued, "We need to be more careful with this *blight* and do a better job understanding it. There must be more to the *blight*."

After they sat for a bit longer, they decided to wrap everything up before the sun began to set. They loaded the cars and went to the house that they secured. Brian talked to everyone as they entered the house, "It was dry around here there was not anyone in sight really, but I think we should keep the same routine of keeping watch, at least three of us always. Eyes on the car, and for anything that may be coming in.

Akim nodded in agreement, "I'll keep watch for the first shift." Apollo chimed in and stated that he would stay up with the first group also.

Brian then said, "Good so we will be the first three, and we will switch out with whoever else is next." Then they went their separate ways in the house to find somewhere to sleep and relax for the night.

Brian and Apollo sat on the rooftop watching the perimeter as they ate snacks, with nothing in sight Brian asked, "So having the *blight* must be a life saver, if I had it maybe most of my friends would be alive. Maybe I could have saved more people..."

Apollo looked off into the distance, "I couldn't say, I never activated mine, I've never been in a situation like Seth for it to awaken."

Apollo put his snack down, "but it must be nice,

as much as we all don't want to admit it, we feared him for a moment. Seth should be dead right now; you saw the ruins he left behind all those runners and crawlers. Seth was already a strong-willed person, but with that blight he became nearly unstoppable."

Brian looked down at his bag of chips, "I see... it was a terrifying sight, I never imagined seeing someone with so much power. People could only dream of being that strong" After some time they talked further about the *Blight*, which only made Brian more interested.

After they switched shifts, Brian went to check on Colby and Bella. He saw that they were sound asleep, so he let them sleep, and just watched. The *blight* being the only thing on his mind as he thought to himself *If I had the blight, I could protect them. I could be stronger, and they wouldn't need to worry about struggling. Seth was unstoppable and was oozing with power, no man should have been able to come out alive. But the blight allowed him to.* After a few hours passed Brian went to the supply stash and retrieved a syringe. As he walked through the house, he saw that Apollo was sound asleep, he slowly approached him and tried his best not to awaken him. He extracted blood from Apollo's arm and rushed out the room. After he returned to the stash of supplies' he put the blood in a capsule and stored it in his bag.

In the morning everyone packed up the supplies they came with and gathered around the cars to talk about further plans. With Albuquerque being the next stop, they were happy to be almost halfway through New Mexico. The group thought the trip was promising at this point, with the amount of progress they'd made. The estimated time of arrival to New Jersey with the minimum number of stops, and long trips should be less than a few weeks if they pushed hard enough. As they kept that in mind everyone seemed to be in better spirits and began to make their way to the next destination. Throughout the drive just like all the times before, nothing and no one was in sight other than corpses and abandoned cars.

Albuquerque, New Mexico

It's been roughly nine weeks and finally they approached Albuquerque, New Mexico, just as they saw on the map, the area was loaded with buildings, which meant there should be people, if not that at least stores to find supplies. While they drove through the city to find somewhere to park Seth and Akim noticed there were a lot of dead men, who were either shot to death or just killed, but they didn't think too much of it at the time. They parked the cars inside a parking lot which seemed isolated.

Ena discussed the plans with the rest, "Seth you are staying here to watch over the cars, while we go out in groups of twos."

Seth was surprised, "But why? If you're worried about my injuries, I'm perfectly fine. The Bligh..."

Ena cut him off, "You are sitting this one out, no debating. Besides leaving you here, allows us to have bigger teams out searching for supplies and these areas seem to be more infested considering the density of the area so we are safer in numbers. No one without a *blight* can stop you and even with the *blight*, they would have to be skilled."

Seth was silent and went along with the plan, while she continued, "Group one will be, Diana, Isis, Akim, Brian and Bella. Isis needs to get used to this world and learn how to survive more, and while doing so, with her knowledge you guys should be able to find more medical supplies that we wouldn't know of. While group two will be the rest of us, Me, Tomie, Apollo, Akim, and Colby. We will find what we can and be back in an hour. We can't stay here too long this place maybe crawling with roamers and maybe even revenants."

Akim spoke up on the topic, "I don't know if this is out of the ordinary but ever since we got here, I've seen a lot of dead men, some seemed to be killed by other humans, bullet holes, and abnormal slashes. Some of the group did not understand what he was saying, and Apollo couldn't understand the direction he was taking this.

"We've seen many dead bodies sadly, so why mention it now, doesn't really seem any different from the normal."

Seth chimed in, "because throughout the trip we've seen all types of dead bodies, ranging from children to adults, men and women."

Seth rubbed his chin and covered his mouth, "Something is wrong here... somehow could those things be forming a hunting pattern or maybe we are just overthinking it." With the eerie feeling of the unknown in the air, they decided that it was best to make this stay as fast as possible. Roughly twenty minutes through, Seth grew bored as he munched on snacks, and paced around, shadow boxing. Group one had already made decent progress, with minimum struggle. They found medical supplies, alongside some gas for the cars, and decided to make their way back taking a different route. After a few blocks, not too far off from the parking lot, Isis noticed a big hotel with military trucks, cars, and containers near the building, with a car that pulled up and escorted people in, "Guys look at that hotel over there that must be one of the military bases, we should go there and see what we can learn."

Diana agreed, "sounds good, but we shouldn't mention the *blight*, or what our objective is, let's get in and out."

Bella said, "I'll rush back to Seth and wait for the others to return to let them know we found the military. The parking lot isn't far off from here."

Brian grabbed her shoulder before she ran off, "Be safe, we won't be long."

By the time Bella made it back, group two was already waiting and looking over the supplies they got.

Seth realized the rest of the group didn't come back and was worried, "What happened to the others? Why are you the only one that made it back?"

With everyone now focusing on Bella who responded, "They are fine don't worry I came back on my own. We found a hotel nearby, it seemed to be the military, so they wanted to check it out, and I decided to come back and inform you all."

Everyone was a bit more at ease, Tomie responded, "We didn't find too much, most of the stores on our end seemed to be raided; but Akim and Seth did have a good point, most of the corpses seem to be of younger to older men, no children, no women. It is kinda odd."

Ena added, "we will wait here for them before we leave, for now we should try to relax."

The rest of group one made it to the Hotel, armed guards were at the front, some wearing military outfit while the others were just in regular clothing. One of the men started asking questions while other men circled them, "Where are you all from? We haven't seen people like y'all around here." The guys checked out the women and glared at the men.

Akim answered, "We are just passing through, we saw the military trucks, so we thought we would pass by for help, and answers."

The men looked at each other and nodded, "Right, come on in, we have supplies and many rooms to stay in, as long as none of you are infected you are welcome."

The men let them in with one leading them inside as the others trailed behind them. As they made their way through the hallway they saw more men, some in regular clothes and others in military attire, giving off dirty looks. By the time Akim noticed what was going on they knocked the group out and tied them up. They separated them. Akim couldn't move and noticed his arms were tied behind his back and strapped to a chair, he was battered and bruised. All he could hear were the voices of a few men who laughed, and talked, "this kid is a great punching bag, I'm surprised he isn't dead yet."

Voice two, "Yea we might have to bring out a crowbar for this one." The men continued to laugh and talk, "After we beat em' to death, we can let some of the other guys use this other boy, while we switch and have some fun with the girls."

Akim coughed up blood, "guys check this tough bastard out he woke up again. These two motherfuckers came here with those new girls. I can't wait to try em out."

Akim noticed that Brian remained unconscious.

Akim struggled to speak "Leave them out of this, don't touch my friends."

One of the men grabbed a bat and swung at Akim's stomach with all his might until he threw up.

"Shut the fuck up kid, no one asked for your input."

Akim began to reminisce about his past, "not so tough without your dad huh?!"

As he thought about his past Akim saw himself being surrounded by some of his old bullies, "Hold him up, so I can get my hits in." One of the bullies struck him with a bat repeatedly until he curled up to the ground.

"Get up pussy!"

Akim was being kicked as he heard someone in the distance yell, "BACK OFF!"

Some man in a suit walked in unfazed by the sight of his son being jumped, "Akim get up and fight back I didn't raise you to be weak."

Akim's father now looked at the boys, "How about you boys stop being bitch made like yuh fathers and fight like men."

The bullies now circled Akim, and his father looked at him, "Get up, I didn't raise a bitch, get up and fight now, FIGHT, OR DIE HERE! FIGHT, FIGHT, FIGHT."

His father's voice slowly faded into a woman's' voice that whispered in his ear, "kill, kill, kill, kill them all, isn't that what you want."

Brian woke up to see Akim laugh like a maniac, almost like a wire had snapped in his brain.

Diana woke up in a dark room to the sounds of girls who cried for help. When her vision adapted to the darkness, she realized there were multiple men who mounted on and forced themselves onto the girls around her.

"Take this bitch and be quiet."

Diana struggled to get her hands untied from behind her back, she looked around for Isis.

She heard a man in the distance, "Look at this

one, she's one of the new ones that came in, looks like I'll be her first."

Another guy pushed him out the way, no I want dibs first, move!"

While they argued they tore off Isis clothes as she woke up. When she realized what was happening, she began to cry.

She struggled to get a few words out, "Diana please help me..."

The men were still talking, "I'll take the front, you take the back then we'll switch."

Diana's heart shattered; everything froze for a moment. Another man hovered over Diana and was getting ready to rip her clothes off, "she's really exotic we got lucky today boys."

In the parking lot the group realized that it was taking longer than expected and they decided to go check on the rest of them. Ena told Seth to stay put, while she took Tomie, Akira, and Bella with her. No one disagreed with the plan, so they followed Bella to the hotel, while Seth stayed on guard near the cars.

Diana could only hear the men laugh and find joy in what they did to girls. She could only see Isis in need of help. Diana snapped out of the rope they had bonded her arms with. She grabbed the trachea of the man hovering over her and ripped it out, which left him gasping for air as his blood splattered everywhere.

"I'M GONNA KILL ALL OF YOU!"

Her Sclera turned black, and her iris seemed to be like the endless colors of the universe.

Brian was tied to a chair and was not able to help Akim. One of the men laughed, "he finally snapped, hell we finally broke the motherfucker!"

Akim continued to reminisce. His father handed him a gun from his coat after he won his fight. "Now Kill them, Kill them all. The fight is not over until the other person is no longer breathing."

Akim remembered how he pointed the gun at each bully and hesitated to pull the trigger. His father turned his back and said, "Are you really that weak, to hesitate is a sign of weakness, pull the trigger NOW!"

Akim looked at his attackers in the present situation, the other guy reached for a gun, "let's put him out of his misery."

Akim laughed uncontrollably and ripped himself free. He pounced on the nearest person, and with the first punch, his head was demolished. Even after he punched the guy's head open, he continued to punch at what remained. He used so much force it made the floor crack.

"Is this what you wanted dad!"

The other guy shot at Akim, which had no effect. Akim looked up, his hair barely covered his eyes. Brian and the other men saw nothing but darkness with a glimmer of the cosmos.

"We gotta' get the fuck out of here!"

One of the men grabbed the bat and swung it at him, but the bat just broke in half after he hit him. Akim grabbed his arm and tore it off. He then proceeded to choke him to death. He used one hand to snap his neck as he tossed his body to the side, with his newfound power Akim rushed toward the other guy who tried to run away. He dragged the man through the wall, and after the dust settled it was only scraps of his body that remained. Akim found himself in the hallway with a bunch of men who were shocked at what they saw. Akim laughed which could have been mistaken as crying at this point, with all his built-up anger, and stress he scratched his scalp and made his head bleed, "Shut up, shut up, SHUT UP!" The men start to reach for machetes, guns, and any type of weapon they could use to kill him.

Diana charged headfirst at one of the men near Isis and used her mouth to tear his throat out. The man struggled to breathe as he gargled on his blood. She then grabbed the other guy and tossed him on his back. She ripped into his stomach, while he grabbed at her arms to try to stop bleeding as he cried out for help. The girls began to scream at the sight of Diana's violent nature. The men tried to swarm her; but she was strong. She was able to punch and kick through all of them. She left no man standing, and after she killed all the men in that room, she walked back over to Isis to check on her.

Diana held Isis's face with her bloody hands and tears flowed from her eyes, "I will never let anyone hurt you. I'll always be here to protect you."

Isis then held Diana and watched her slowly pass out. "I know, and I really do appreciate you for doing what I can't", she whispered right before Diana closed her eyes.

Ena and the rest finally made it to the hotel, and saw only two people outside, "Hey are you guys' military?"

The men looked at each other smiling, "Yea, do you need shelter? If so, you all can stay here."

The men heard screams from inside of the hotel. "Wait here we will be right back."

They walked away and left Ena and the rest outside for a moment. When they entered, they saw Akim drenched in blood, killing their men one by one. Bodies were torn apart everywhere; you couldn't even make out what he did to some people. After they heard the gunshots in the building Ena and the others rushed into the hotel, to see Akim laugh and cry in pain as he talked to himself. "Are you proud of me now, I fought, I didn't back down, I FUCKING KILLED THEM ALL!"

Tomie tried to get his attention, "Akim relax, we are here to help." She reached out her hand towards him, "Just relax."

Akim tackled her to the ground and tried to swing at her face. Tomie's *blight* activated at her will. She shoved Akim off her and kept him at a distance as if he were a wild animal.

Akim paced slowly back and forth, "I'm not weak, I'm not a pushover."

Tomie stood her ground ready to defend herself from Akim. He charged at her recklessly, which forced her to hit him with a side kick that sent him rolling into a wall. Akim struggled to stand up, so he kneeled, taking deep breaths, as he looked up in front of him. As his vision became blurry the last thing he said was, "Tomie?" before he closed his eyes from exhaustion.

After quite a bit of time passed, Seth thought it would be best to meet the rest of the group at the hotel. Once he entered the hotel, he saw Akim, and Diana unconscious, while Brian and Isis were slightly injured. The hallways were covered in blood and dismembered body parts. They left the building to discuss the situation at hand. They stood in front of the hotel, and everyone looked defeated. When Akim finally woke up he filled them in on the situation, "This was a trap, it wasn't the revenants for the random number of corpses of men. The men here must have been ex-military and random survivors. They killed off all the men, took advantage of the girls and women. Diana held Isis as she began to cry and shake. Seth began to grind his teeth and clenched his fist, while the others were sick from the thought of what happened.

Brian added, "By the looks of it, if they didn't kill the men on the streets, they tortured them to death. If it weren't for Akim's and Diana's *blight* we'd be dead right now."

Ena was discouraged, "So what do we do now they need our help we can't just leave them here."

Seth got angry and walked away, "well we can't keep sitting around either. We keep wasting time! If that's not bad enough we keep ending up in these shitty situations, our people could've been killed, and worst Isis and Diana almost got raped!"

While Seth walked away, Akira saw that the group was mentally and emotionally in shambles. Everything moved in slow motion for Akira in that moment, he looked at Isis and remembered the time he was too weak to protect her.

Akira mustered the energy to grab Seth, "No we can't just leave them here to die!"

Seth glared at Akira and pushed him off, "We can't waste time here either, they already did enough! They need to learn how to survive on their own."

Akira was on the floor, while the others listened to Seth in silence, "DID YOU ALL FORGET THE MISSION, THE ONLY GOAL WE HAVE IS TO GET TO NEW JERSEY! Once we get there, we can save the world properly! We can't worry about everyone else's problems right now, when there's a bigger goal!"

Akira got up and his eyes teared up out of anger. He attempted to shove Seth who didn't budge, "Who's gonna' fight for what's right!? Who's gonna' help these people survive?!"

Akira was more amped up and punched at Seth who still didn't budge. "We are all fighting for our lives, and no one is ready to die. Who's gonna' fight for the weak?! Akiras' knuckles bled from punching Seth's almost brick like body, "Who's gonna' make kids believe they've got a hero?!"

The others were too exhausted and fatigued to even stop him. Seth glared at Akira and responded, "You wanna be some type of hero all of a sudden, this has been the world for years. Let me ask you something, all those years you were in Japan what did you ever do to help anyone, while you played games, went to school, and lived a comfortable life? Did you ever consider the people out here who were starving and dying out of injustice? What about the people who were being kidnapped and sold into sex trafficking?"

Seth pointed at Isis and said, "Out of all of us here she is the only one who has done anything to actually help people out of the kindness of her heart, but now that the sad reality of this world is in front of you, now you want to be some kind of hero." Akira glanced away while the others stayed silent. *He knew Seth wasn't wrong with what he said.*

Seth continued, "No one other than Isis did anything to help the world until the problem was in front of them."

Akira responded, "You're not wrong, but that doesn't mean we need to leave these people here to die." Akira grabbed Seth's collar "You have the power to save everyone, no one can stop you! No one here is as strong as you. I-I could only wish to be anything like you." Akira suddenly swung at Seth's face and landed a clean punch, Seth realized he was bleeding.

"So how about we fight for what's right! If we truly want to save the world, we must do it step by step, day by day, and regardless we will make it to New Jersey."

Akira sclera now filled with darkness and his iris shone like the stars in the solar system. Seth struggled to firmly grab his wrist so he wouldn't continue. Akira noticed he didn't hurt himself after striking Seth. He looked over to the car window and saw his reflection, his eyes reminded him of the universe surrounded by darkness. Seth pushed away Akira's hand and wiped the blood from his nose. Everyone was in shock that Akira had finally awakened his *blight*, and everything went silent for a moment. Seth saw how passionate Akira was about the situation at hand, and although he was angry, he was also calm knowing that he wasn't completely wrong.

Seth walked back and stood in front of everyone, "As much as I hate this idea, he isn't wrong. We can't just up and leave people behind, and we also can't leave anyone for dead." Seth looked at Akira, "From here on out our goal is still the same, make it to New jersey. While doing so we will save who we can and make cities safer for the living. We as a group can do anything, and no one can stop us. So, I guess it's fair to take it into our own hands to rebuild this world. Step by step, day by day."

Akira and the others smiled when they saw Seth change his mind. Seth looked around, and noticed that the busses, and military trucks nearby seemed to be in good condition.

"First, we need to sweep the whole hotel, check for survivors, and once everyone is accounted for, we need to find a place where they can set up and build, even though we are helping everyone doesn't mean we have the luxury to stay and babysit anyone. Akira, Akim, and Ena, come with me to sweep the floors, everyone else stay out of here and stay on guard." They entered the hotel and split up to cover more floors efficiently top to bottom. The top floors did not have much to show, only small belongings and personal items from whoever was there last. Halfway through the hotel Seth found rooms filled with girls and women, with barely any clothes, some bruised. Seth explained to them that they are all safe and he will get them out of here. Akira saw rooms filled with corpses, blood on the walls, weapons covered in dried up blood, and teeth and bones on the floor. Akim came across rooms with more women, bruised, beaten, and some not even moving. He tried his best to comfort them. He let them know they were now safe, and they would be leaving this hotel. Ena went through her floor, and noticed a bunch of kids, some dead, while others were blindfolded. She had to back out of the room for a moment because she couldn't hold her tears in, *this world is cruel.* Gathering the energy to approach the children, she took off their blindfolds and told them everything would be okay. Back on the main floor Seth saw the room Akim busted out of, and the massacre he committed, "I never would have thought we could cause so much damage.

Seth looked over at Akim and looked around, "They deserved it, you were defending yourself, the best thing I can say is don't sweat it, you did what you needed to survive... It's that simple."

They got out of the hotel with a bunch of girls and women covered in sheets or random clothing, and a few kids on the side. Seth checked the military containers. They were filled with food, diesel, gas, clothes, water, and other medical supplies. Seth directed everything and told Ena and Tomie to hand out water and food to them. He asked the rest to load the cars, and buses with supplies.

Seth talked to Akira while they are loading the bus, "We got really lucky with all of this, the military must have had all kinds of supplies sent out around the country."

Akira smiled while he passed the supplies over, "We did... and thanks for listening to me."

Seth stacked the supplies inside the back of the bus, "I don't truly agree with you, but you're also not wrong. I thought about it, what's the point in having all this power and not use it to help others."

Diana spoke to some women and one of them

informed her about a safe location, "If you guys are looking for a safe place, Santa Rosa is where one of the military camp sites that should still be up. I heard one of the men talk about it, and by the looks of it that's where they got most of these supplies."

Diana took what she learned and brought the information to Ena and Tomie. Ena realized that Santa Rosa was the next stop for them also, "This works out perfectly, when we are done here, it will take roughly two hours to get there. These people can finally have somewhere safe to live until all of this is over."

Tomie's smile faded, "This all sounds good, but do you really think we can make it? Even with the *blight*, I feel as if things are only going to get worse from here."

Ena gripped Tomie's shoulder, "Look around you, we've been through a lot, and look how many people we have saved so far."

They took a moment to watch everyone they saved, eat, talk, and even the quiet ones who looked as though they were in peace, Ena continued. "As long as we are all together, we can do anything, and there is nothing in this world that can stop us."

Once they finished packing the vehicles, they informed everyone about the trip ahead of them to Santa Rosa, and the plan to bring them to safety. With everyone being so grateful for everything they'd done so far; they listened and began to line up to get inside the buses.

Ena asked the others, "We need two people to drive the buses, who will drive?"

Brian and Colby stepped up, Brian laughed a bit, "We don't know how to drive a bus, but it can't be that hard. Lead the way and we will be right behind you guys; it should be a straight shot."

With that being settled they took off, finally leaving that trap. They made their way across the state without any hiccups. Roughly two hours had passed when they finally arrived. It was just before the sun started to set. As they approached the entrance to the city, they saw military trucks driving everywhere, guards on duty, and tents filled with people in the distance.

Santa Rosa, New Mexico

They pulled up to a few guards who were standing at the perimeter. The guards asked them to park and explain where they were coming from. Ena got out the car to do the talking, "We just saved these women and children from a trap, coming from a city about two hours from here. One of the women mentioned that there would be a military base here. So, we came with the hopes of finding a place for them to stay."

One of the guards went to check the buses, while the other explained the processes for entry. "After we check all of you for infections, we can escort everyone to tents and treat them with the proper care."

They got instructions to follow one of the guards to some containers. After they made it, they separated the men and women alongside the children. They were told to enter the containers. When they entered, they were instructed to throw all their clothing away, shower and sanitize. After showering, female guards inspected everyone one by one. Afterwards they were handed some sweatpants and a pair of shorts with two gray shirts per person. Throughout the checkup Akim realized all the bruises, cuts, and few bullets that landed, were almost completely healed. Once they finished up and everyone passed inspection, they were all guided to the center of the camp where people were talking, laughing, and eating dinner. They were guided to the kitchen tent where they received their food. The group was surprised at how organized and safe this area was compared to what they'd encountered earlier. Some of the women they saved, came to thank the team again for guiding them to safety and they wished them well. Moments later one of the guards silenced everyone to get their attention.

"Today we gained more allies, and we grew as a community. It was brought to my attention that these brave individuals saved multiple lives and are here with us." He pointed a cup in the group's direction smiling in joy. "We honor your bravery and commitment throughout these hard times."

Everyone clapped and cheered for them. The group was overwhelmed by the attention. Some had light tears of joy while others expressed shock.

Seth lifted Akira's hand, "This kid right here is the real hero!"

Everyone cheered even louder, some of the survivors came over and picked him up. When everything settled back down people asked about the hotel incident and wanted to know how they prevailed. Seth left the area with the hope that he could speak with their leader. He asked a few guards where he could find the leader of the base, after some time he finally made it to the General's container. Seth entered to see a man sitting at a desk full of papers, and communication equipment on the side of him.

Seth asked "How long has this city been set up? Everything here seems to be safe and foolproof." The General looked up from the paper, "Ever since the start, when we got word of the *Collapse*, military centers have been set up throughout most of the country. Alongside any other country we could reach." He stood up and walked towards Seth. As he reached for his hand he said, "You kids did a good job out there. You all could make a great addition to our forces. We heard what happened there.

Seth walked halfway to shake the General's hand. "Thanks, and we appreciate the offer, but we can't stay here. We mainly came here to drop off the people. I came to ask for supplies for our long trip."

The general laughed, "Why would you want to go back out there, you all are safe here, and we grow in numbers."

Seth replied, "This is one of the safest places ever since the *Collapse*. But our goal is to save people and create a haven to restart the new world."

The General turned his back and looked at a map, "So you're serious... We can't force you to stay, and you will always be welcome here. As far as supplies go, we saw everything your group came with, and we can trade off items."

Seth nodded in agreement, "Sounds good, how about this. You keep the buses, diesel, and medical supplies we picked up, in return you give us more military food, gasoline, and a few guns, nothing too much, a few pistols, assault rifles and a decent amount of ammo."

The General turned around, "Sounds good, I will also supply you with a map of where there should be more bases as long as they didn't fall." Seth shook the General's hand once again and thanked him for the help.

Chapter VIII

WHERE ARE WE GOING FROM HERE?

Later that night they all grouped in the same tent to talk. Seth broke everything down to them, "I cut a deal with the General, we will be getting more supplies and some weapons before we leave tomorrow, he also gave me a map of other military locations."

Tomie spoke up, "What's that look on your face then. What are you thinking about?"

Seth looked at the group alongside Colby and his people. "We just never had anything like this, and it would be nice if we could stay. But I know our goal is to get to New Jersey." Seth clenched his fist, "I wish I was strong enough to do this alone, so you all didn't have to go through anything else. But this is a journey we all must venture through together. Brian, Bella, and Colby, as much as we appreciate you, I can't allow you three to continue."

Brian was shocked, "but why, I thought we were in this together, just because we don't have the *blight* you think we aren't of use or something."

Seth tried to calm him down, "No, this simply isn't your fight. We got our own battles to fight, and you have yours. Stay here, be safe and help them expand. You guys can probably convince them to start going back to Arizona and saving the rest of your old group."

Colby said, "We came this far because we want to save the world. We knew the risk and-"

Bella cut him off, "No Seth is right. The only reason they survived that hotel was due to Akim and Diana. We knew what we could be capable of but, we don't have the luxury of having that power to rely on. We can help more here, and not be a liability to the primary goal at hand."

Brian bit his tongue, he knew this was best for his friends, "Fair enough, I believe in you guys. We will do what we can here."

Seth and his group felt some of the weight lift from their shoulders because they knew this was the best play.

Colby now stood in front of Seth and stuck out his hand, "Just promise you all will come back alive, there is no room for failure."

Seth shook his hand and said, "We will, we don't have a choice." Bella and Brian said as they made their way around to say their goodbye. Seth continued, "Try to rest well tonight, this will be our last day in New Mexico, next stop is Amarillo, Texas." Reality swept over the group, when they realized they must go back out there and move forward. No plan b, no alternative, just one simple goal that felt harder to accomplish day by day. They separated, going to their tents, preparing themselves for the long journey.

Sometime that night Diana became restless, and stroked Isis' hair, "I think you should stay here. It would be safer for you."

Isis turned towards her, "I'm not letting you guys go out there by yourselves, this is a team effort. I don't have the right to hide behind the military while you guys are fighting for your lives." Isis looked into Diana's eyes which made her feel at peace, as if she were staring into the endless abyss of space and held her face, "I don't want to leave you behind. I will be just as strong as you and the others."

Diana held Isis's hands, "I don't want to lose you out there." Isis tried to comfort her, "You won't. Like Ena said, no one out there is as strong as us. No one and nothing will be able to get in our way." Shortly after the conversation Diana fell asleep while she held Isis.

With the sun finally out and clear skies the group got ready to leave the military post. The General had all the supplies ready to see them off. Once they loaded the cars people waved them off and they were on their way to Texas.

They passed through some of the small cities in New Mexico. The only sight to see were abandoned buildings and, corpses everywhere. There was no sign of life. It all sank in once again; this was their reality. After some time, they arrived at Tucumcari, New Mexico and stopped for a bit to stretch and eat. Everyone grabbed some food and water while they sat in silence.

Seth said, "since we are good on supplies, we can just relax for the time being. After we finish up here, we can make it to the next stop and try to keep the same structure. Drive, find somewhere to stay for the night and keep moving forward."

Akim got up, "sounds good, I'm going to go take a piss." He walked off behind some random building unzipped his pants and used the bathroom. Akim did not realize there was a roamer in the distance that was coming toward him. He finished up and looked around. That was when he noticed the roamer. The hotel incident sparked some type of anger inside of him, he walked toward the roamer and kicked it to the ground. He stomped its head in, and after he destroyed its head completely, he continued to walk. From the corner of his eyes, he realized there were a few revenants in the distance that were amped up and screaming. Akim came back to his senses, he rushed toward the group,

"Guys we gotta go, there's revenants around!" By the time he tried to warn them, there were roamers and revenants coming from buildings. They all rushed to the cars and left whatever they were eating behind. They pulled off and ran over a few of them when they did. After a few wrong turns they detoured and got back on track getting out of the city. During the drive they saw an abnormal number of abandoned cars on the road along with roamers. They stopped a little past San Jon, New Mexico after they were in the clear, and tried to understand what was going on.

Tomie said, "for us to see roamers is not unusual but revenants are usually people that just turned right?"

Ena added, "That is true. By the way we almost got swarmed, a lot of people must have died... we just missed the chance to save them. This virus spreads like a wildfire."

Diana said, "We gotta get out of this area asap. We don't know what caused it and this is not a situation that needs to be solved right now."

Everyone agreed to get back into the cars and leave. Seth led the group. He drove off but what he didn't realize was that his tire had nails inside it.

Glenrio, Texas

As they approached the Texas border, in the split second it took Seth to take his eyes off the road, Seth caught a glimpse of this lady-like figure. At that moment the car tire blew out, which caused the entire vehicle to spin and roll out of control, while the car behind him also swerved and crashed.

Seth was unconscious. While in this state of unconsciousness Seth envisioned himself walking in the woods. As he walked, he could smell burning flesh and hair. The rest of the group followed him. He could sense the groups' discomfort. He looked off into the distance and saw a patch of the woods up in smoke as though it were on fire. The group continued to walk until they eventually approached a charred patch of the forest. Here they saw burned bodies, from children to adults, scattered along the dry ground with brittle burnt rope still around their necks.

"What kind of monsters could have done this?" Isis cried out while pointing above them.

Tomie was also unconscious. Like Seth, she saw herself in a vision. She was being dragged by her hair while her hands were bound behind her back. All she could see was darkness because something was over her face, and all she could hear was the excited chanting and cheering of the crowd. She was momentarily rendered blind by the sun when the bag was taken off. She looked up to see a crowd of people laughing and grinning as she had a rope thrown around her neck without warning. She slowly rose, as struggled to breathe.

Akim, who was also unconscious, had a vision that they were in a city with a few scattered tall glass buildings, surrounded by a pack of revenants. He was out of breath, and struggled to carry Seth, as they looked for a way out of the city.

Diana, who was unconscious, was in the middle of what appeared to be a desert-like area handcuffed, on her knees, and surrounded by soldiers, one of whom was pointing a gun at her head.

"The general said we should only bring some of them back alive; this bitch killed too many of our men."

Akira also unconscious, had a vision. He saw himself as he emerged from a small tent. He observed strange people pass him as he silently followed them. Akira remained behind a tree and observed the strange group of people gather in front of a person who wore a robe as they reached a small lake. The woman removed her robe and looked directly at him. What Akira saw shocked him because the woman's sclera was empty and devoid of light; but her iris shone purple as if she had the *blight*.

Seth awakened soon after his brief unconscious state to a loud ringing sound in his ears, blurred vision, and blood on the side of his face. He crawled out of the car and into the harsh sunlight after he broke through the windshield. The dreadful groans continued, and darkness crept in. After a few minutes he finally regained his focus and noticed a swarm of undead approaching. Seth looked in the car. He hoped to see his sword but instead he saw that it was broken in half. Diana, who was also in the car, struggled to get out of the wreck.

He assisted Diana out of the passenger seat, "C'mon, it's a horde in our way."

She stood and brushed herself off before she said, "I'll get them, go check on Tomie, and the others!"

Tomie kicked out the front windshield and helped Akim out, Seth ran to the back door and ripped it off.

"Help me get him out!" Akira demanded since Apollo was still unconscious.

After Seth got everyone in the car he turned his attention to the horde, Akira asked, "What's the plan?! We can't leave them here, and we don't have any of our weapons!"

Seth walked towards the horde, "We go right through them, we have no choice but to stand our ground here and kill 'em all, DON'T LET ANY OF THEM GET THROUGH!"

Seth closed his eyes for a moment to focus, after he thought about the hotel incident, and what Hannah did, he opened his eyes. His sclera was swallowed by darkness and his Cosmo colored iris shined brighter, he pulled a knife from his pocket and cut into his arm which forced him to bleed. Everyone was shocked seeing the blood flow down his arm change from red to black as he held out his arm the blood flowed to his hand forming a sword. Akira was speechless. *What is the blight truly capable of? He had just manifested a weapon with his own blood, and activated the blight of his own free will.* Seth rushed at the first layer of the horde and proceeded to hack and slash at their necks and heads. Diana stood over Isis and Apollo who were still unconscious. Akira watched Seth in awe and thought, So *this is the blight a weapon, a tool of destruction.* Akim stayed back to take care of Ena who was still out cold. Tomie's heart raced as she watched Seth tear through the roamers. She watched as he was slowly being surrounded. Her breathing became heavier, and her pupils dilated. She grabbed a piece of broken glass from the wreck, and rushed to help Seth, her sclera turned black, and her purple Cosmo colored iris shined as she used the glass to cut herself. Her blood faded into black and flowed to her hand, it then formed a scythe. Tomie decapitated the roamer that was trying to claw at Seth's back, then she leaned against Seth's back to cover all the blind spots. Seth turned his head and nodded. He led the assault against the last dozen roamers. He sliced two of their heads off at once, while Tomie followed up and ripped five roamers in half. Limbs and torsos were left scattered on the ground. Seth continued to fight as he thrust his blade through one of the roamers' mouths and pierced another. He kicked both to the ground. Tomie finished the rest by spinning her scythe like a fan and using the force to chop down the last three roamers. She planted the hilt of her scythe into the ground, as it slowly faded into mist. Seth's sword faded into mist as he looked over at Tomie and nodded.

"Thanks, let's check on the others."

The darkness in Seth's and Tomie's sclera faded back to white as they walked over to the others. The others were still unconscious and laid in the shade of the car wreck.

Seth asked, "Are they alright?"

Diana replied, "Yea, they are breathing, just knocked out from the wreck."

Seth looked around at the cars, "Alright, we won't be able to carry them, we need to give them time."

Seth walked over to Akim, as Ena began to wake up. "Good they're awake, the others are still out, and the cars are completely wrecked. We need to get to safety for now."

Akim nodded and asked, "What's the plan?"

Seth replied, first get Ena to the others so she can relax for now. Then we need to gather what's still usable. The plan is to still move forward." Seth stated, "We have no other choice, but to keep moving forward."

Akim saw that look in Seth's eyes, and it was pure confidence and anger. He replied, "Understood."

Akim picked up Ena and brought her over to the others as Seth started dragging bags and supplies out of the wreck.

Akira asked, "So what's the plan?"

As Akim carefully put Ena down she thanked him and replied, "Seth said we will keep going, right now we are seeing what we can carry with us, I'm assuming sooner or later we can find a car or something."

Diana tried to change the mood and said, "maybe we could find some bikes. they don't run out of gas, and we don't have to worry about another accident."

Tomie chuckled a bit agreeing with her. "Akim, let's go help Seth gather supplies, Akira and Diana stay here with the others."

They nodded, as they started to strip the car of supplies, Akim asked, "How did you activate your *blight* like that, with such control."

She shrugged, "It just came to me, I felt something in my heart and bam! My *blight* is activated. It felt so natural, kinda like learning how to walk, the more you do it the easier it is."

Akim asked, "What about the scythe, and that sword that you two manifested."

Tomie was silent for a few moments before responding, "I really don't know, It just felt right, as if I already knew how to do so. Especially after Seth did it." She looked over at Akim and asked, "How did you activate your *blight*, like what were you thinking about? We knew it took ambition, but it had to be more than that."

Akim said, "It was a bit foggy, but I recalled the time my father forced me to fight my bullies, after he had watched me not fight back. He didn't let me leave until I won, and then he forced me to kill them. I was being beaten by those men in there and snapped the moment I recalled pulling the trigger."

Tomie finished grabbing what she could, and looked over at Akim, "Geez, that's insane. I

171

thought I had it bad, I was pushed around for being weak, but I never had to deal with it to that extent. Mine activated the same way when I sparred with Seth a second time. I thought about all the people that laughed at me at different points in my life. I thought about how people considered me weak, and I just snapped."

They sorted out the supplies and separated duffle bags and backpacks.

Akim looked over at Tomie and said, "So that's what it is, ambition and anger. Once we find somewhere safe, we need to discuss this with the rest of the group. If we all have access to our *blight,* we would be in a better position."

Tomie nodded, "You're right, let's see what Seth got so far." They walked over to Seth and saw him pack medical supplies. Tomie asked, "So how is it looking, we see some potential supplies that we can take with us but, we will have to leave some of this stuff behind."

Seth turned around and stood, "You're right we will have to decide what's more important, most of the weapons are still here, the only one that broke was the bow that Isis was using." Seth walked over to the supplies and continued, "The smartest thing to do is for each of us to carry a duffle bag with supplies, and a backpack filled with necessities. Until we find some other form of transportation I'll lead the way, you two will keep guard on the sides, Diana will guard the back, while we keep Isis, Ena and Akira in the center. That will help us maximize our defense capabilities."

Akim nodded, as Tomie added on, "Seems about right, the ones in the center can carry all the important items, like the medical supplies, canned foods, water, and ammunition. Everyone else can carry things like the jerky, a few bottles for our-self, some ammo, clothes, and maps."

Akim and Seth agreed, Seth said, "Let's get this sorted out, we all have to carry guns also, everyone will have their own pistols, with those on the exterior also carrying a rifle. We will shoot as a last resort. We can't take the chance to be swarmed."

Once they were done plotting, they stored the supplies they could and went to check on the rest of the group. When they saw that everyone was awake, they discussed the plan to the others. The others agreed to the plan, and they began to pack for their next destination.

Seth said, "This won't be an easy walk but there's a gas station in Adrian, Texas. Our best bet is to get there and bunker down for the night."

The walk started well, they gained some distance on the highway road, using shirts to keep the sun out of their face. After they had walked ten miles all that seemed to be left was stranded cars, and corpses. Ena and Isis grew tired and struggled to keep their pace with the others.

Isis, struggled to keep going, and said, "We gotta stop for a bit, this heat is insane."

She plopped down in the shade of a car, followed by Ena who was also sweating profusely, "Yea, how much longer do we have to go."

They were all sweating but the ones that had the *blight* showed no signs of exhaustion from the heat. They all took shelter in the shade of the cars, while Seth looked off into the distance only to see waves of heat.

He took out his map. After he looked at it, he said, "We got about another ten miles until we reach that gas station. We can stop here for a bit and push through the last three hours before it gets dark." They ate some snacks and drank water.

Once they cooled down Tomie mentioned the conversation she had with Akim. "So, we came to the conclusion that it wasn't just ambition, you also need anger to trigger the *blight*."

They all looked at each other than looked at Seth, Ena said, "let's start with Seth. What were you thinking about when you activated your *blight?*"

Seth looked up into the blue sky and responded, "I didn't want to lose, I thought about all those years of training with my father, and failing repeatedly, and yea I snapped. I didn't want to lose to Tomie or Diana."

Diana looked at Isis and said, "I saw what those men did to the other girls and women in that hotel, and when I saw the same thing happen to Isis, I lost control."

Seth looked at Akira and asked him what made him so angry. Akira responded, "Part of me was mad at myself because you were right...Then I was mad cause' out of all of us you are undisputedly the strongest. Yet you didn't want to help those people. I know I'm not weak but compared to you, I don't stand a chance. It's more like hate with a mixture of disappointment... If I had the power you possess, killing wouldn't have to be the first option."

Isis responded with a sudden burst of energy, "So that's what it is" everyone looked at Isis as she continued to speak, "Hate, anger, the yearning to be able to surpass your boundaries is what activates the *blight*."

Seth looked at Apollo and thought to himself. *There must be more to it, Apollo wanted this more than any of us, so why can't he activate his blight.* Apollo sensed Seth's gaze, which made him look over at him. Seth changed his focus back to Isis and the others.

Ena replied, "That leaves me, you, and Apollo. We need to find our trigger. If we all have our *blight*, that would put us at an advantage."

Seth looked at the sky, and then off into the distance and replied, "Yea she's right, we need to figure it out, as of now we need to keep going so we can have some walls around us and plan our next move."

They picked up their bags and supplies and kept walking. They walked past stranded cars, the bodies of failed survivors, car seats covered with blood, and flesh scattered on the highway. This was all they saw for miles.

Chapter IX

BLIGHT II

With the sun about to set, it grew cooler. Seth saw a gas station in the distance, "We're almost there. Once we get there we'll bunker down for the night and always have two people on guard duty."

Everyone nodded, as they continued walking, when they got to the gas station, they checked around the building and looked for threats and hazards. With nothing in sight, they went inside and found most of the store was looted with several items scattered throughout. They laid their supplies down and barricaded the front doors. Tomie looked at the damaged shelves and ripped a few off the hinges, "we can go climb that ladder on the back of the building and start a small fire on the roof."

Akim replied, "Sounds good, we can also keep watch up there."

They gathered some matches, papers, and more wood shelves and brought them to the roof. A beautiful mix of color appeared in the sky as the sun went down. They got a fire started and everyone sat around it for warmth, eating small amounts of rations.

Seth started the conversation, "I'm going into the nearby city, while you guys' rest here. We need some sort of transportation, to keep going on like this." Seth paused for a moment and looked at Tomie. For a moment, he felt as though he could feel her emotions and he continued, "I will try to find some vehicles that we can use and if we are lucky in the morning we can head out in cars and not have to walk."

Akim replied, "I'll go with you, I know how to hot wire some cars, if we can find decently older models even without the keys, we should be fine."

Seth nodded, "So it's settled me and Akim will head out shortly, this isn't a group decision. Just take this time to relax."

The group looked at Seth, and Tomie replied, "We know how you are, and how you'll go about things. We can't stop you and won't try. You do what you think is best for the group. Just be safe."

Seth nodded and looked at Tomie. He sat in silence and tried to understand this odd connection between him and Tomie. He could feel the concern in her heart as if they were connected.

Adrian, Texas

After some time, Seth and Akim arrived at the nearby city. They stayed low to the ground and darted from building to building. Akim noticed a school in the distance and a court filled with tents, "That looks like an abandoned military camp, they may have some cars left behind."

Seth nodded, "Alright let's make this fast, if this place is really abandoned it may be revenants around."

They kept the same pattern of running building to building and checking their corners. When they made it to the front of the school they saw cars, and military trucks, that seemed to be in good condition.

Akim saw guards on the rooftop, "Wait this place is not abandoned, there's guards on top of the buildings."

Seth replied, "The last base seemed really nice, and the leader was generous, maybe they could help us out."

Akim replied, "It doesn't hurt to try, what's the worst that can happen?"

They walked out the shadows with their hands up, shouting, "Guards!"

After a few seconds, the front doors opened and a few soldiers came out pointing guns at them, soldier one asked, "Are you guys infected."

They shook their heads saying no. The soldiers put their guns down and gave them instructions, "The moment you get inside, go to the cleansing room, and after that we can get you situated."

Seth spoke up, "We have been traveling from Arizona and just came from New Mexico, we need to talk to your General."

The soldiers looked at each other and soldier two asked, "How are the other states' conditions? Our communications can't reach out of the state, and Texas so far has been one of the safest states. With the most military outpost still standing from our knowledge."

Seth replied, "Arizona looked like a massacre from what we encountered, and New Mexico was semi ok. We saved a huge group of people and guided them to safety somewhere in Santa Rosa where there is a strong military base that seemed to be safe. The general there gave us supplies and sent us on our way."

Soldier One asked, "So where are you guys going, and why do you need to keep traveling when you should be seeking shelter?"

Seth looked at Akim and replied, "That's why we need to talk to your general."

Soldier One replied, "Head to the cleansing area and we can prepare our general for a meeting."

They were escorted inside, seeing classrooms filled with survivors. Many slept, and others sat restless. They entered a room where they were cleansed and checked for any signs of infections. After they were finished, they got dressed and were escorted further down to the principal's office where the General was located. They looked at a map on the wall that showed all the safe havens in the country.

Soldier One said, "Here are the men that wanted to talk to you."

The general faced the map, and he turned his head to the side to speak to them, "I see, stand guard at the door." The two soldiers saluted and left the room, while Seth and Akim stood in front of his desk. The General walked over to his desk and waved his hand at the seats. He insisted they sit. After they sat, the General started the conversation, "So I heard you requested some supplies, and you're traveling through the country. For what? Why would you not seek safety until all of this is over. Why didn't you guys have stay with the people you saved?"

Seth looked over at Akim and he nodded, Seth replied, "We need to make it to New Jersey to make it to-"

The General spoke over him, "Dr. Hex huh, you aren't the only people to think of him, but New

Jersey is considered a no man's land alongside a few other states. As you can see it's not a secret the CDC failed to come up with any answers. So, we contacted other high-level scientists in any field and tried to bring some of the greatest minds together, but they only managed to scratch the surface. Sadly Dr. Hex was the only person we couldn't reach."

Seth replied, "that's why we need to make it to his University."

The General raised his voice, "Boy did you not hear me, New Jersey is a death sentence. No form of military was able to get in, so what makes you think you can?"

Seth replied, "Dr. Hex assigned us an experiment. It was to improve our physical capabilities. But I'm assuming it worked better than he expected. We are stronger, faster, and more capable than anyone or any weapon you can think of."

The General laughed, taking off his hat and running his hands through his hair; he replied, "I don't think you understand what you're up against, just because you saved a few people doesn't mean you can save the world, or make it to New Jersey. We've lost hundreds of men trying to make it to New Jersey alone. We've also lost thousands who tried to set up camps and safe zones around the world." The General glared at Seth and continued to raise his voice, "AND YOU THINK YOU'RE GOING TO WALK IN HERE AND TELL ME, YOU'RE MORE CAPABLE THAN AMERICA'S MILITARY."

Seth chuckled and replied, "Actually yeah, and I'm willing to put my life on the line to prove myself. Tomorrow, if I can beat twenty of your men armed with knives versus me with my bare hands you have to supply me with everything that I ask for. You underestimate us. We saved dozens of people in that hotel, and we survived countless hordes already and came out alive. You think you could compare us to those men and women you call soldiers."

The General raised his eyebrow and replied, "Us?" The General finally looked into Seth's eyes, "I can see it in your eyes, you're not bluffing. How many people are in your group? How many of you were a part of this experiment?"

Seth replied, "There were eight of us, the others are held up in a nearby gas station. We came here to find some cars and supplies. But after we saw your men standing guard we decided to simply ask for help. The other base was generous, so we were hoping for the same hospitality here."

The General stood up and replied, "Prove yourself to me tomorrow and I'll give you all the information and supplies you need."

The General put his hand out as Seth replied, "Sounds good." Seth shook his hand.

The General said, "We will pick up the rest of your friends early in the morning when it's safest. For now, you two will stay in one of the rooms and in the morning, we will test your strength."

Seth shook his head and replied, "No we will be back in the morning, I'm not leaving my group over there by themselves."

The General looked at him and nodded. "Understood."

They arrived back at the gas station and saw everyone resting, as Diana and Tomie kept watch.

Tomie asked, "How'd everything go?"

Seth replied, "We ran into a military camp, and decided to talk to the General. He was reluctant to give us supplies, but he has a ton of info on New Jersey and said that it's a no man's land and doesn't think anyone could make it through. We will prove ourselves tomorrow, and I'll explain everything else when we head over to the city."

They all stared at the fire while they sat under the night sky. Seth prepared himself mentally for the morning. When the sun rose, they packed their supplies, and started to make their way to the city following Seth and Akim.

Seth said, "So we are heading to a military camp. I made an offer to show the general our power and get supplies in return. Once they see that we are capable of surviving, they will have to supply us with items, and give us information."

Ena replied, "Do you think it's the best idea to be telling these people of the *blight*. The whole purpose of us being in Arizona was to stay away from the public eye."

Seth shrugged and replied, "What's the worst that can happen?"

Isis joined the conversation, "Right, they also seemed nice, we haven't had problems before with any of the other bases, and they lent us supplies for our journey. I think we'll be ok."

Ena replied, "You could never be too careful, the other military bases didn't know what we were truly capable of. Power can corrupt people... we've seen it throughout history. The end of the world doesn't change the nature of people."

Seth glanced over at Ena as they continued to make their way to the camp.

They finally arrived at the front door of the school, seeing soldiers standing guard and kids playing around in a fenced area.

Seth stood in front and said, "We are here to see your General. He should be waiting for our arrival."

Soldier number one walked over to Seth and replied, "All of you follow me to the cleansing room. Then we will proceed to the General."

Seth looked at the group and nodded. They followed the soldier inside and were separated with the men going to one room while the women went to another. Both groups were checked for scratches or any signs of wounds. Once they were checked in, they were handed a change of clothes. Now they wore military cargo pants, with dark green shirts to match. While walking through the hallways and passing different classrooms they saw some people clean and fold clothes, some kept track of supplies, and some were with kids who survived after the *Collapse*. They were directed outside to a parking lot where they saw tents, crates of weapons, food, and other supplies. Military vehicles could be seen in maintenance, and soldiers were training. Soldier One instructed them to stay put, while he made his way to a tent. Shortly after that soldier came out with the General who stood in front of the group, "So you weren't joking. If you can prove yourself, I will honor what I offered you."

They followed the General to the center of the parking lot and he screamed, "Attention!"

All the soldiers stopped mid-task and stood behind the General properly lined up at attention. The General turned to his soldiers and said, "I WANT ALL OF YOU TO SHOW THEM HOW STRONG THE MILITARY IS. DON'T HOLD BACK, AND THE FIGHT DOESN'T STOP UNTIL ONE SIDE ADMITS DEFEAT."

The soldiers roared, as Seth turned to his group and said, "I got us into this mess, and I'll get us out of it."

They nodded, while stepping back from the center of the parking lot. The General stood in front of Seth and said, "There will be no use of weapons, this is a test of your strength, and I have to make it fair somehow."

Seth replied, "Well me with my *blight* versus your soldiers isn't a challenge, just stand back and watch me. The General stepped out of the center, and thought to himself, *blight?*

All the soldiers whispered amongst each other, "He really wants us to fight one person?"

"No way are we supposed to fight some random civilian."

"Look at this cocky bastard."

The General stepped out of the center and said, "Fight as you please, and attack in waves. Fight as you trained and don't embarrass the United states military. FIGHT!"

Seth stood his ground as the first row of five people approached. Soldier One was a few inches taller than Seth, and slightly more muscular as he stood in front of the others and said, "Let me take care of this."

Seth taunted him to start the fight. He smiled and closed his eyes. Soldier One took offense and charged at Seth in haste, he threw a punch that Seth dodged and followed with another that allowed Seth to close the gap and open his eyes. With his sclera now being dark as night and his eyes imitating the colors of the universe, Seth hit the soldier with a fast three punch combo to the chest and a power shot sent him rolling on the concrete back toward the other soldiers awaiting to fight. The General and other soldiers were shocked to see Seth dominate his first opponent with such power; the other four soldiers surrounded Seth in a box-like positioning.

Seth fixed himself to face one of the soldiers who yelled, "COME!"

The soldier that faced him charged and threw the first two punches that Seth evaded by stepping back. The soldier behind Seth proceeded to put him in a full nelson.

The other soldier cheered, "Yea get his ass!" "Finish him now!"

The other two soldiers closed in and grabbed his

arms and tried to restrain him while the one in front tried to close in for another assault.

Tomie asked the others, "Do they really have a chance to win? They got him pretty good."

Apollo shook his head and thought about how Seth rose out of the hospital covered in blood and replied, "I don't think anyone can stop him. He's a one-man army."

Seth lifted his head up, looked to his left and right and saw the soldier approaching him. Seth jumped and hit the soldier that approached him, with a drop kick that made him slide across the ground. Utilizing the support of the other three soldiers that were entwined with him, he landed on his feet and followed up with a right kick that freed his arm and sent that soldier rolling. Then a left kick freed his other arm and left that soldier curled up next to him. There was one soldier who struggled to hold on to Seth.

He screamed, "Get in here and finish him!"

This time ten people ran in to help. Seth quickly broke out of his grasp and grabbed the man by his shoulders. He threw him at one of the soldiers that charged at him. Now with nine left Seth took the offense, by fighting the closest soldiers. He hit the first soldier with three quick body shots and grabbed his shirt with both of his hands stacking him back into another soldier as he followed up with a side kick which sent them both to the ground. The third soldier tried to take the assault by throwing a heavy punch that Seth redirected which made the soldier slip behind him, while he parried the fourth soldier that tried to follow up. Seth continued as he grabbed the fourth soldier by the neck and lifted him up effortlessly. The soldier Seth grabbed looked into the universe of Seth's' eyes and his vision grew blurry right before Seth dropped him and left him on the ground as he gasped for air. The other soldiers were reluctant to approach him and the third soldier that was behind Seth tried to get him with a sneak attack. Seth fell to one arm and kicked the soldier straight in the stomach which made him kneel on the ground and vomit. Seth stood over him as the other soldiers stood still in fear.

The General walked over and called the fight off, "You win... You proved your strength. I haven't seen someone fight like this before."

Seth closed his eyes took a deep breath and smiled, when he opened his eyes the darkness in his sclera faded back to white. All the soldiers that didn't fight helped the ones who were injured after fighting Seth.

Seth and his group followed the General back to his office, so they could gather information for what was to come, as well as get some supplies for the trip. The General pulled some folders and reports out of his desk and spread them across the table.

Then he said, "You held up your end, and I feel like I need to introduce myself properly now. I am General Rize." Each folder was labeled, "Revenants," "The *Collapse* Protocol," and a black folder labeled in white that read New Jersey. Across that folder was a red stamp that said, "Mission Rejected."

General Rize leaned on the Desk and said, "These are all the files we have for the *Collapse*, and those damned monsters. If you have any questions, I'm an open book."

Seth picked up the New Jersey folder and saw papers of soldiers that were M.I.A, deceased, or turned. While he looked through the folder Ena picked up the other folder labeled "The *Collapse* Protocol" and skimmed through the plans and procedures that the military had for the world. What she read astonished her; *We are sending batches of each branch to all corners of the world. We attempt to save as many civilians as possible. Hold off, expand, and wait for the Collapse to end. We still have no real information of how this started or how it's going to end. We are the last hope of the world, and if we give up on our people this will be an extinction level event.* Isis picked up the "Revenant" file as Diana and the others watched her flip through the papers. *To kill these things properly aim for the head. It's not just infections that force people to "turn." No matter how people die they will turn. Bites, scratches, and the revenant's blood can speed the process of the inevitable. "Turning" can vary from person to person from seconds to even hours. Completely dispose of dying people who are not capable of recovery before they "Turn." The CDC had no information, and other talented scientists couldn't figure out the origin. The only thing that was confirmed was that this virus cannot be cured with our current knowledge. Some call it nature's wrath...*

Seth looked at the group after reading a line from the files and turned to the general and asked, "So Dr. Hex is really our only chance at surviving this mess?"

General Rize nodded and responded, "and even then, that's a stretch. But seeing what you are capable of. If he created that power, you all possess, I personally believe he can solve this virus."

Diana asked, "What are their weaknesses? We don't have time to sit and read all these files."

The General replied, "They seem to have none. People that turn, start off really aggressive and seem almost impossible to fight back, if you don't have some form of weapon. And if you aren't physically ready, they will overpower you, they aren't capable of holding back like us humans. So, to answer your question they don't have a weakness. But once they run out of people to feed on, and are left alone for days on end, they become weaker, slower, and less capable of posing a huge threat alone. As you see in those papers, headshots, or any strong hit to the brain should work. I wouldn't recommend traveling at night because those things are dangerous, and it's harder to know what you're dealing with." General Rize walked over to Seth taking the "New Jersey" folder out of his hand and continued, "other than that, I don't have any real advice. I can only tell you to know that New Jersey is the most dangerous state, those revenants over there are restless and more aggressive." General Rize walked back over to his desk and took his hat off, "That's why we believe Dr. Hex may be the answer. It's almost like this virus is defending that state, not allowing any of our forces to penetrate deep enough to reach his school. Even if you guys are strong enough to get there, you still have to worry about getting infected. Understand that Dr. Hex is in one of the most dangerous parts of the earth right now, we are all putting our trust in that he is still alive."

The room grew silent. Understanding that Dr. Hex was truly their last hope Isis spoke up, "We don't have a choice if he is dead or not, we must try. We are the only ones that can make it that far." Isis looked at Seth and continued, "Seth already survived being infected, so I know we are all capable of surviving infections."

Diana glared at Isis, and General Rize stood up and replied with a sudden burst of energy, "WHAT!? Do you know how long we've been looking for some sort of lead on how to stop this virus? You're finally telling me now!"

The group looked at each other and put their attention back to General Rize as Seth replied, "Well how would that help anyone. We are still trying to figure out the full extent of our powers."

General Rize replied, "I would have been more eager to help you, I already see what you are capable of, and I could tell you were holding back. But with this new information we can change the course of the *Collapse*. We don't have to play defense anymore. With your group as our spear and shield, and the supplies and number of the military we can save the world." Seth thought to himself for a moment and looked at his group. They all seemed happy about the suggestion, *This would be good for them, and power in numbers, endless supplies, we can do this.*

He turned back to General Rize and put out his hand, "We can do this, I was already unstoppable, and with your forces and supplies we can't be stopped."

General Rize shook his hand and replied, "Yes, we can, but you do have to prove to me that you won't turn. After that I will arrange plans for us to leave by tomorrow."

Seth nodded and replied, "I can manage that." General Rize replied, "Your group will stay here, and we will keep this information strictly between us for now. We can't sway the emotions of people until this is proven and then we can arrange plans for the next step."

Seth stayed with General Rize while the others were escorted to a classroom that seemed to previously be a soldier's living quarters. Six neat bunk beds, and crates of supplies alongside the wall.

Soldier One said, "If any of you need food or water there are chefs in the cafeteria. And feel free to roam around the school or parking lot." He closed the door and left them while they settled in.

General Rize said, "There are a few houses with revenants that we never got the chance to clear out. When we get there, we will kill all but one, and let it infect you. After I've confirmed with my own eyes that you don't turn, I can arrange plans today, and we can leave tomorrow."

Seth nodded and replied, "I'll follow your lead."

Chapter X

UNITED WE STAND

Seth and General Rize stood in front of a white house, the clouds partially covered the harsh sun, and the noise of the undead moaned and scratched against the walls. General Rize took in a deep breath and dropped the duffle bag he carried.

"Alright I'll approach from the front, and you go to the back, we kill all but one."

General Rize pulled out his machete and started towards the door.

Seth stopped him, shook his head, and replied, "Just stay here, I'll take care of it."

Seth walked up to the door, and kicked near the locks which sent the door flying. He turned to his left and saw two roamers in the living room. He then turned to the right which revealed one in the kitchen. He picked up a bat he saw on the floor and walked over to the living room as the two roamers struggled to attack him. He swung at the first roamer and hit it on the head which sent its' entire body into the wall headfirst. He then swung on the second one and busted open its head. That roamer collapsed from the sheer force of Seth's swing. He turned to see the other roamer slowly make its way toward him, Seth walked closer to the door and let it follow him outside, as he rested the bat on his shoulder he said, "We got one."

General Rize replied, "you're one smug bastard."

Seth smiled, as he walked near a tree and replied, "Well, let's get this started."

General Rize opened the duffle bag, dug out a rope, and some gauze. He rushed over to Seth and helped him tie the roamer against the tree. Seth zoned out, as he stared into the roamers' lifeless eyes.

General Rize stood on the right a few feet away from Seth and pointed his pistol at his head, "I can't take any chances."

Seth looked at General Rize and nodded, as he proceeded to reach his arm out in front of the roamer and shoved his forearm into its mouth. It clenched onto his arm which forced him to scream. Seth took his arm out and punched its' skull in repeatedly with the same arm until its' head was completely destroyed and cracks were left in the tree.

General Rize took a few steps back, and kept his gun pointed at Seth while he asked, "Talk to me, you good son?"

Seth looked at his arm and replied, "Yea, it just hurt."

General Rize picked up the gauze and walked over to Seth so that he could wrap his arm. While General Rize wrapped his arm he said, "You don't feel weak, or hear voices yet?"

Seth replied, "No. I'm fine. Like I said, we are immune."

General Rize looked off into the distance and laughed, "I never thought we'd see the day. We don't have to hide in these cities giving people false hope of survival, we have an actual lead after all these months." Seth nodded as General Rize continued, "There are a few things we must discuss, when we get back to the school. For today we will instruct everyone to pack tonight and get ready to head to one of the main bases in Texas before we march forward to New Jersey."

General Rize picked up the duffle bag and led the way back to the school.

Seth said, "I understand that we are immune, but earlier you said, all the other scientists couldn't even comprehend what this virus is. So worst scenario if Dr. Hex is dead... what's after that."

General Rize laughed and replied, "Well now we

have a lead, and other than Hex, we have all the scientists located in a main safe zone in PA, Atlanta, and Oklahoma. They will lock you up, see what makes you guys tick, drain your group of all their blood to make vaccines, maybe even find a way to obtain those powers you possess."

Seth glared at General Rize and started walking slower falling behind him. General Rize stopped walking and looked at Seth. He saw that his joke made Seth uncomfortable and stopped laughing, "Listen, I was just joking, we wouldn't need to go that far. We just need some blood samples, so we can run a few tests, nothing to jeopardize you or your friends' lives."

Seth nodded and continued to walk as he replied, "My group has already been through a fair amount of bullshit. Their safety is the only thing that concerns me."

General Rize thought to himself, *I've seen that look before, was he going to kill me just now?* As they continued Seth looked at his eyes in the reflection of a car window and noticed that his *blight* didn't fade away like last time.

He thought to himself. *How is this even possible?* With the short walk they finally made it back to the school. The moment General Rize got to his office he ordered the survivors and soldiers through the school communications system to gather in the parking lot. The survivors asked the soldiers questions while they made their way to the area, "What's wrong?"

"Do we need to evacuate?"

"Are we being attacked?"

With the soldiers being just as confused as the survivors they responded with vague answers as they tried to keep everyone as calm as possible. "It's just a meeting."

"Keep calm and follow the line."

"We are fine, this is one of the safest states in the country as of now."

"Just get to the parking lot and calm down." Seth made it to the group and followed the crowd outside, then he told them.

"We are good to move on, General Rize said we will be making plans to push to New Jersey, With their forces and supplies, and our power, we got this." Tomie saw Seth's bloody bandages, and looked away in sorrow, while the others seemed happy that something was finally going in their favor.

They stood in the back of the crowd and watched General Rize give his speech, "I know this is without warning, but I am proud to announce, we are going to a bigger facility in Amarillo, Texas. More supplies, more people, and more protection, with that being one of our strongest outposts. We received orders to transport all survivors there. We will be leaving tomorrow, as of now I want everyone to pack what they can and be prepared to leave in the morning. I can't take any of your questions at this time; but I will say, we've got a plan to save the world, and our odds just got better. So, I want you all to be at peace knowing that THE MILITARY WILL NOT SURRENDER, WILL NOT BACK DOWN, AND WILL NOT CRUMBLE!"

The soldiers in the crowd cheered, and the survivors followed suit. The group seemed to be in better spirits, with Diana being the only one who was not impressed.

When the survivors and soldiers left to go count people, and pack supplies, General Rize stayed outside with the group to discuss the plan.

Diana stated, "You got everyone riled up, but what's the real situation at hand?"

General Rize replied, "For one, I was telling the truth, Amarillo Texas is one of the safest places in the state, and I can't leave these people here without some form of a leader. Our first goal is to get these people to safety. Second, we must gather soldiers and supplies throughout the trip. We also need to make sure the survivors we have now stay alive and have enough supplies while we make our way to New Jersey. The more people that stay alive are less people we must kill because they are infected once everything reverts to normal. Just because we have a lead, doesn't mean we can divert from our main plan of keeping safe havens for both soldiers and survivors. Like I said, we must play offense and defense now. Third, our only option for scientists other than Hex are in Oklahoma, PA, and Atlanta."

Everyone except for Apollo and Tomie were confused, so Diana asked, "What the hell is PA?"

General Rize was surprised by the question and Apollo replied, "Pennsylvania, it's a state close to New Jersey."

They all replied, "Oh ok."

Tomie chuckled and informed General Rize, "They are from outside of the country."

After a moment, the General continued, "Well now that's cleared up, I believe getting the scientist from Oklahoma and Pennsylvania will prove to be our best option, since Atlanta would be too far."

They nodded in agreement, as he continued, "And once we get to Pennsylvania, we will let them take some of the blood samples, while we march directly into New Jersey mowing our way through to Hex University. With your powers, and our back up, we have a shot at saving humanity."

Diana replied, "If this is our best shot, I'm in."

She looked at Isis who nodded in agreement. With the rest of them also in agreement.

"Me too."

"Same."

"This is our only chance."

Ena asked, "Why don't you just contact the other generals and inform them of what's going on?"

General Rize replied, "I wish that was the case, but we are a smaller safe haven, we don't have any real means of reaching out to other bases like the bigger facilities, they have actual Radios and VHF's Radios, while the smaller safe havens like mine only have walkie talkies, and word of mouth information. Once we get there, we will be able to really get the ball rolling."

Ena replied, "I see, so tomorrow's the big day."

General Rize turned his back to the group and said, "Yup for now be prepared for tomorrow and get some rest tonight. This may be the last time you get to rest well. We already know the revenants aren't the only problems. We will have to fight the people that gave into insanity, do things outside of our nature, fight the unknown, alongside being prepared to make sacrifices. All of this to save the world."

After he walked off the sun started to set, and each member of the team slowly realized General Rize was right. It wasn't just revenants they had to worry about. It was the twisted nature of humanity, a world without government, and even when there once was a government, was it any different?

The group returned to the room that was provided to them and talked about what they needed to be prepared for.

Tomie leaned on one of the walls and said, "We still have to be careful, even with the military support does it really make that big of a difference."

She looked at Seth's arm as Diana sat on one of the beds next to Isis and replied, "She's right, all of this sounds nice on paper, but we've passed many fallen camps, these people won't be any different."

Seth stood in front of the door and replied, "They didn't put us on the front line."

Diana replied, "We shouldn't be here, there's a reason why Dr. Hex kept this information isolated."

Isis tilted her head and joined the conversation, "Some things we have to be transparent about, none of us here are scientists, or are capable of creating any form of a vaccine, if this is one of the only ways to save the world, I feel like it's necessary we take the risk."

Ena agreed and said, "Diana you're right about the risk, but this is honestly our best option. Did you have something better in mind? Do you think we can just march to New Jersey and enter that death trap with no knowledge of what to expect? And now we won't just have the military, we will also have other scientists to do research on the *blight* serum."

Diana stood up and replied, "That's the main problem, what do you think they will do with the power of the *blight?* It's the reason why Dr. Hex went so far to put us in a private resort and told us to only stay in contact with him. Just look at what we've done so far and what we are capable of with the *blight.* Do you think we need random people to be walking around with that kind of power?"

Seth looked at Akira and replied, "If that's the price to save the world, then so be it. We will have to deal with one problem at a time."

Diana looked away, and everyone else agreed that neither of them was wrong, but what choice did they really have. To let the world fall apart from hiding their power or giving the world a chance and dealing with the consequences later.

When they awoke, they heard groups of people talking and walking in the halls, knowing what the plan was, they got their supplies, and prepared to leave. They left the room to join the horde of survivors following them to the parking lot. Once they reach the exit, they saw soldiers, command people onto different buses, doing head counts, and storing supplies in some of the military vehicles. They looked around and saw everyone in good spirits, because of the speech the General gave. Those few words of hope and encouragement went a long way, as they watched kids that hadn't boarded the buses run around, laugh, and play.

Isis said, "This is what we are doing it for. This is why we risk it all. For these people and others like them, the ones that still have hope, the ones that cry at night, the ones that gave up, and the ones that wait for a miracle. They're waiting for us."

Isis smiled and walked off, she headed over to General Rize as the group looked at each other and followed her lead. General Rize greeted them and introduced them to a few people from his platoon.

"These are my most trusted soldiers, y'all will ride with them, I know you all don't need protection, but we can't risk any casualties in your group from here on out."

They hopped on the back of a military transport vehicle as General Rize continued, "Realistically, I don't know the first thing about vaccines or how this works, so it's better to have all of you there when we need you. We leave shortly, we expect roughly a fifty-minute drive."

They nodded as he walked off, to support his other soldiers, and assist other survivors.

After some time, the driver knocked on the rear window and said, "We are ready to depart."

They heard several school buses and military vehicles pull off, and one at a time each one honked their horn as they left, to signal the others to follow. In no time they passed Vega, Texas. The group started to talk amongst each other.

Diana asked, "So what's the plan if something goes wrong? We will be surrounded by layers and layers of soldiers."

Isis replied, "Can't this just be the break and assistance we need, how about we trust someone other than ourselves for once and go with the flow."

Ena joined the conversation, "It is better to be safe than sorry." She looked at Seth, and Tomie and continued, "Seth and Tomie are capable of manifesting weapons, and the only people who have not activated their *blight* are Isis, Apollo, and me. As long as we stay together, we should be fine."

Seth nodded and replied, "Yea, no one can stop

us, as much as I trust this General, if push comes to shove. We will kill them all, and keep moving forward, and revert to our original plan to get to New Jersey."

The group grew silent for most of the ride because they knew that Seth wasn't bluffing nor over exaggerating.

Amarillo, Texas

They reached Amarillo, and it was empty and quiet.

Apollo said, "Isn't this place supposed to be one of the biggest military bases in the state? Where is everyone?"

They got deeper into the city and saw a bunch of survivors walking around as if it wasn't the end of the world. Supermarkets, now a food and resource outlet that was run by soldiers who were giving out supplies to people that were lined up. Kids ran around and played freely. Elders walked and took in the nice weather. After a while the truck came to a stop. They tried to figure out why they were stopped by a military vehicle from this city.

General Rize explained himself to the soldiers and stated, "We are here in search of refuge, and I need to speak to the general here."

The soldiers looked at his badges and nodded,

they let him pass without much question. They continued to drive deeper into the city and saw more military equipment as well as rescue helicopters. Some were loaded with weapons, trucks, crates, and tons of other supplies. They saw soldiers training, and even survivors being trained for combat. The group was in awe when they saw the raw power of the US military.

Isis asked, "Do you guys really think we can fight all of this, if it was necessary."

Diana sat in silence, looking at all the supplies, and the countless number of soldiers. They entered the gated area where each bus was checked before they were allowed through. The buses with survivors were escorted by soldiers to a different location, while General Rize and the group were sent to the heart of the base to meet the general of this city. They finally made it to their destination. When they got out of the vehicles, the group and General followed a soldier into the airport.

They walked around the airport for a short time and entered a room where they saw seven other generals all seated at a table. A map of the country was on one wall that showed different states, and the threat level of each. New Jersey was at the top of the list for highest threat, alongside Tennessee and Oklahoma, they also had paper scattered on the table. They stopped talking, and turned their attention to the group, and General Rize.

The soldier said, "This general came from a different outpost, and had some important information regarding new plans. A new strategy."

The generals nodded and the soldier left. General Rize said, "I came here to present to you this group of people, subjects of Dr. Hex, they are immune to the virus, and possess powers beyond us."

The council of generals looked at each other in disbelief as he continued, "I've witnessed with my own eyes, this man right here getting bitten by one of those roamers and has not yet to show any symptoms or signs of turning. To my knowledge this is his second time getting infected. They also are more physically capable than any soldier we have. With their powers and our resources, I request that we change plans and make some form of attack.

The council of generals asked the group, "What is it that you possess, what is this power that separates all of you from the rest of us?"

Seth looked at his group and turned back to the council replying, "it's a serum created by Dr. Hex to overcome the boundaries of our human bodies. It's made us stronger, faster, more resilient, and simply more capable of surviving. At first an experiment for human advancement, and now this is our last chance to save the world. He entrusted us with this power called *blight.*"

The room grew silent, and the generals looked at each other and then at Seth as they realized that none of this was a joke.

Chapter XI

DIVIDED WE FALL

The Council of Generals called for soldiers, who came to escort the group out. General Rize said, "Listen, they will just ask tons of questions, but I promise you, I will do everything as planned, just wait for me and let me do all of the talking."

The group nodded as they were kindly escorted out of the airport and to a nearby camp filled with containers, tents, and more soldiers. They all received their own tent near each other, which had cases of water, snacks, (MRE) Meals Ready-To-Eat and a bed.

The soldier that guided them said, "These are your quarters, you are welcome to walk around to each other's tents just stay in this location that was provided to you until you are instructed otherwise."

They nodded as he walked away, Seth looked at Diana and saw that she was still uncomfortable he said, "Diana I know how you feel, but let's bear with them just for a little bit. This could be the factor that changes everything."

Diana looked around and replied, "I just don't trust them, if this plan includes us, why can't we be in that room talking to them right now."

Seth and the others sat in silence for a moment and Ena replied, "You're right, but you know how these people move already, they try to keep things away from the public, and probably didn't want any of us to scare the public with everything they have going on. I don't think any of us fully trust them, but this is a risk that we must take."

Diana sighed, and replied, "I just have a bad feeling about them that's all. If you all are taking the risk, I'm here with you. I'll be patient."

Meanwhile the Council of Generals were discussing ideas. General One said, "We will lock them up, we can't allow them to leave. If they are the key to stopping the *Collapse*, we will rip them apart and make a vaccine."

Some of the generals nodded, while General Rize rebutted, "No, we can trust them, they mean well. They already saved countless lives, while making their way to New Jersey. Don't you all understand, if we work together, we can penetrate our way into New Jersey and make contact with Dr. Hex."

One of the other generals stood up punched the table and replied, "We can't allow it, we don't know how any of this started, and if they are immune to the virus, wouldn't that mean Dr. Hex may be one of the main reasons why the *Collapse* happened? Do you know what could happen if we decided to let those lab rats get back to Dr. Hex?"

General Rize responded, "Do you really think someone like Dr. Hex would want to destroy the world? He has no reason to do something like this. Why are you all hesitating to make the right decision?"

The council just looked at him in silence with no emotion as he continued, "We don't even have any of the proper scientists here so what good will it be to have them chained up and useless when we could be fighting on the same side."

General Three replied, "We have enough supplies and people to make it to a scientist, that's not Dr. Hex. Oklahoma was overrun and is also a no man's land, so we won't be able to reach that scientist who is most likely dead. If they are immune to this virus, Dr. Hex is now our number one suspect, and this means New Jersey is ground zero."

General Rize was surprised that the whole council wouldn't even consider supporting them, and replied after a long pause, "You don't want them as enemies. We wouldn't be able to stop them."

The council laughed as General One responded, "Are you underestimating the power of the US Military? How dare you stand here and try to take their side."

General Four glared at him and responded, "The decision is made, we will capture and detain them. We have doctors here that can poke at them and see what makes them tick. If we can acquire this *blight* for ourselves, we will turn the tide of power and be able to show true dominance with an iron fist."

General Rize from Adrian, Texas stood there watching his plan slowly wither away due to the ignorance of his fellow leaders. Disappointment replaced all the hope and plans that he had for this journey, with the choice already being decided; he knew he had to warn the group at all costs. The room grew silent, as the council just stared, one of them called for guards. Right before he could make a run for it, two guards restrained him. They grabbed him by the shoulders and forced his arms behind his back. The council instructed the guards to assign him to a room and keep him on watch. They left while the council created a plan they called *'blight Extraction'*.

The sun was beginning to set as the group waited in their tents for further instructions. Diana laid on her back as Isis laid her head on her arm and they talked.

Diana said, "A world where everyone has the *blight*, wouldn't that be a terrifying thing. You saw me kill those men in that hotel. We saw the hospital that Seth destroyed then walked out drenched in blood. The bloodbath Akim left behind in the hotel. Should anyone truly be capable of such power?"

Isis replied, "We don't even know if it will get that far. Like Seth said, we must deal with one problem at a time. Best case we can make some sort of vaccine that allows immunity, worst case it will grant them immunity and the power to possess the *blight*. But what other option do we really have?"

Diana sat in silence just staring at the top of her tent for a moment and responded, "You guys might be right, we will have to risk it all just to save humanity."

Seth entered Akims' tent and watched him doing push-ups, Seth asked, "Do you think this is a good idea? Do you think we can trust the military?"

Akim stopped and sat on the floor took a deep breath before responding, "So far, they did right by us, and they mean well, I think we can trust them. But Diana isn't wrong either, we only scratched the surface of the *blight*, and yet look at what we're capable of."

Akim looked at Seth and said, "But what other

option do we have, either we hide the *blight* and let humanity die off, or we take our chances letting them make a vaccine with the blight, and hope that they can't possess the powers that come with it."

Akim shook his head and continued, "We will find out when the time comes, but for now we must do what we can to save the world. Right?"

Seth nodded and replied, "right" putting his fist out, Akim fist bumped him. After a few seconds of silence Seth went back to his tent sat on his bed, looked at his hands. He thought about what he did to Hannah, how he managed to survive the horde in the hospital. He clenched his fist, thinking about how he can't afford to fail his group.

Meanwhile the council was sorting out plans to detain and extract the *blight* from the group without causing a panic, and what steps to take afterwards.

General One stood up and said, "We will proceed with the operation during midnight. We can't allow them to get too curious on why there is a delay on plans to move forward. We will gas their tents, separate them, and retain them in the basement of this airport. If this so-called *blight* is as powerful as they make it seem, we will need chains, and anything else that can stop them from getting free."

He turned his back from the table and looked at the map on the wall and continued, "After obtaining blood samples, we will kill six of them, reducing the threat level, and leave a male and a female to see what makes them tick." He pointed at Oklahoma and continued speaking, "we lost communication with the scientist there, and the state threat level is too high for us to risk a rescue mission, the number of revenants keep growing, and we have yet to see anyone make it out of there. So, we must assume most if not everyone is infected or dead." Turning back to the table he continued, "We don't have the means of traveling all the way to Atlanta, and Dr. Hex is off the table leaving us to use our resources."

General Three said, "So are you suggesting we run a test here in this city? We have a few doctors and scientists here but not to the same caliber of the ones we lost contact with."

General One responded, "We can't let this opportunity slip through our fingers. We must take action tonight. While they are asleep, we will send out a squad to capture and detain them."

The rest of the council nodded, as their minds were already set.

As midnight approached, the group was already sound asleep, not prepared for the squad that was sent to capture them. The squad swiftly snuck through the tents that surrounded the groups, giving them no room for escape. Once they finally closed in on their targets, they all put on gas masks, and proceeded to throw knockout gas in all their tents. They gave it a minute, after they heard, the groups coughing come to a cease, they ran into the tents, bounded them with chains, and bagged their heads. They carried each of them out of the tents and threw them into the back of the military trucks.

General Rize paced in his room and watched as a group of military trucks returned to the airport. He already had a gut feeling that the group was detained and in those trucks. He walked to the door and heard two guards while they had a conversation. With all this knowledge he knew that this was the perfect time to escape and save the group. He looked around the room, ran over to a desk and knocked everything over as he collapsed to the floor pretending to be passed out. The guards grew silent and peeked inside the door. They saw him on the floor passed out. One walked in to check on him while the other stood near the door.

He kneeled to check his pulse, "He should be fine. I can feel a pulse, but we might need to take him to the medical bay."

The soldier turned around and walked toward

the door, General Rize snuck up behind him and strangled him. He took the soldier's pistol and proceeded to stuff the barrel in the second guard's back, shooting twice. He dragged their bodies to the room, checked his surroundings and looked for signs. He proceeded to follow the signs to the parking lot, and hoped that's where he would find the group.

Seth woke up to the feeling of warm sand on his back, he slowly sat up to see a beautiful oasis in front of him.

He took in the beauty as a familiar voice to the right of him asked, "How'd you sleep?"

He looked over to see Tomie lying beside him bathing in the sun. He responded, "I rested well, and as a bonus I got to wake up to such beauty."

Tomie tackled Seth causing them to roll through the sand until he ended up on top smiling, holding her face. Seth heard the voices of men talking, and bright lights forced him to open his eyes. He looked around to find himself in a basement of some sort bound in chains alongside the other men in his group. He saw people using laptops and a few doctors having conversations with their backs turned away from the group.

Diana woke up to the sound of men yelling, and her being kicked around in the middle of nowhere, the sun was burning bright, and she saw Ena, and Tomie bound in chains, while Isis struggled to get away from two men. Diana was forced to her knees and a man put a gun to the side of her head, she looked at Isis who was crying, and tried to make her way to her.

Diana said, "It's okay... you can do this without me" and closed her eyes which were filled with tears. Diana opened her eyes with tears running down her face and looked around to see the women in the group bound in chains just like her in some sort of basement. She had a moment of relief when she saw Isis was okay alongside the others. She saw doctors and other people who walked around while they used their laptops and wrote notes. Diana looked to the side in disappointment, it turned out she was right about all of it.

General Rize finally made it to the parking lot area to see just a few trucks and guards wearing special op clothes. He checked his gun and saw he only had eight bullets. He knew his odds weren't good against the four guards. *I know for a fact that they are in these rooms, but if I act rash, it may be people inside ready to kill them, I have to play this smart.* He snuck past a few pillars getting closer and closer to the guards. After he made it near one of the trucks, he peered through the windows, and saw a few AR's. He laid his back against the truck as he heard another truck arriving. *If I can't save these kids, humanity won't have a chance to survive.* He peeked around the corner and saw a few people come out the truck and take out tools, and cases filled with medicine and drugs. As they made their way into the room, he caught a glimpse of the girls restrained, and when they entered the other room, he only saw a few doctors and people on computers but assumed that the other half of the group was also in there. He noticed that the guards were not paying attention and he rushed into the truck and grabbed one of the AR's. He checked the magazine and saw it was loaded. He took off the safety and hopped out the truck. He then shot at everyone he could see. He managed to kill three of them, while one soldier ducked and ran behind a different truck.

The group and people in the rooms heard the commotion outside, one of the doctors said, "it can't be a breach down here, what the hell is going on out there."

Seth and the rest of the men struggled to break out of the chains but were still weak from being drugged. Diana and the rest of the girls also struggled to break free while the doctors tried to stay as quiet as possible.

The last Special Ops member fired back blindly, and called on his walkie talkie for back up, "Someone is down here attacking me, all my men are dead. I need assistance ASAP!"

General Rize stayed completely silent while he peeked underneath the truck, He saw the Special Ops officer, switching positions. He pulled out his pistol shooting him in the foot and legs, crippling him.

General Rize ran over to him and disarmed the injured officer as he asked, "Are there any more guards inside or just scientists?" The special Ops officer spit in his face and glared at him. General Rize wiped his face off with his shirt and shot the Special Ops officer in the face, leaving his brains splattered along the pavement of the parking lot. General Rize reloaded his AR and took a deep breath before he kicked in the first door.

He aimed his gun at scientists and doctors; with no guards in sight he demanded, "GET YOUR ASSES DOWN TO THE GROUND NOW AND LOOK AT THE WALL!"

Without any hassle they listened to his commands as they cried in fear.

He looked over at the girls and rushed to get them out the chains, "Listen you all have to go, take one of the trucks that's out there and keep moving forward, get out of Texas, and make it to New Jersey."

After getting the gags out of their mouths, he unbound them from the chains and helped them get out the room, while helping them to one of the trucks.

Isis asked, "What about the others? We can't go without them."

Rize looked at the other door and said, "We will be right behind you, just go, There should be a walkie talkie in the vehicle, change it to channel nine to and wait for us to call you. Don't ever use the first few channels to communicate those channels are most likely filled with other soldiers."

He forced them into the truck, and made his way to the other door, as they rushed out of the parking lot. He ran inside and pointed his guns at the doctors and scientist as he yelled at them, "TURN TO THE FUCKING WALLS NOW."

They listened to him out of fear, as he proceeded to ungag the guys, he said, "I'm sorry it came to this, I didn't think they would react this way. The girls are already out, I told them to only use channel nine if they get their hands on a walkie talkie and avoid using the first few channels since it will be filled with other soldiers."

They all nodded, and Seth responded, "I know you meant well, this isn't your fault."

General Rize unbound them from the chains helping them out. Before they made it out of the door, they heard other military vehicles arrive in the parking lot. Seth looked at the others. His breathing was heavy, and he was still tired from the drugs like everyone else. General Rize peeked out the door to see soldiers getting out of the vehicles and aim their weapons at the doors, while the council of generals stood behind them.

One of the Generals, yelled, "We Know you are in there, and we will not allow these lab rats of Dr. Hex to leave Texas. We will hunt them down before they get the chance to reunite with the man who may have caused the *Collapse*. You all have until the count of five to come out with your hands up. Or else I will kill every single one of you, and hunt down those girls, and make them suffer in the worst possible way until we find a cure."

The general started counting, "1... 2...", Seth whispered, "Follow my lead, and General Rize once we are all out start shooting so we can make a break for it."

General Rize nodded as Seth walked out slowly with his hands up, followed by Apollo, Akim, and then Akira.

General Rize rushed out behind them spraying bullets. Seth and the rest of the guys ducked behind trucks as they tried to find a way inside them. The other soldiers fired back. General Rize got hit in the shoulder by a round as he made it inside the truck the rest were in. Seth sped off. The other generals commanded their soldiers to hunt them down, "MAKE SURE THEY DO NOT MAKE IT OUT OF TEXAS, WE NEED A FEW OF THEM ALIVE!"

As Seth made his way out of the parking lot, he was followed by other soldiers. He saw that the path ahead was cut off which forced him to go north, he said, "The girls must have gotten away, but we need to regroup."

General Rize replied, "We will later, right now worry about shaking them off of your tail first!"

Seth clenched his teeth and glared into the rear-view mirror; he saw four military trucks tailing them but not shooting. He looked at the others and could see they were still fatigued from the drugs. Seth continued to look at the soldiers in the rear-view and his sclera became swallowed in darkness.

He looked over at general Rize and said, "Take the wheel now! I'll handle them."

General Rize nodded and switched seats with Seth as he drove. Seth opened the door, climbed to the top of the vehicle, and pounced onto one of the military vehicles. He broke through the windshield, grabbed the driver by the throat and snapped his neck with brute strength which forced some of the vehicles that were following to crash and come to a halt.

General Rize looked in the rear-view mirror and asked, "What the hell is he thinking?"

Akira yelled, "Stop the car, we can't leave him behind!"

General Rize came to a stop, and they all rushed out of the car to see Seth rip the guts out of his first victim. When Seth noticed the other soldier he blitzed him, he punched him twice and caught him by the neck with one arm as he forced him to his knees. As the soldier coughed up blood and struggled to get out of his grip, he looked into Seth's terrifying yet oddly calming purple nebula eyes.

The other six soldiers from the wreck pointed their guns at him, while the lead soldier yelled, "Put him down now!"

The lead soldier shot, causing Seth to use the soldier he was choking as a human shield. The rest of them fired their AR's, and Seth threw the soldier like a ragdoll, at one of the men as he rushed at them with astonishing speed. Seth forced his hand through the first soldier's chest, and smiled as he crushed his heart, he followed up by grabbing the hole he just created in this soldier's chest and ripping him in half.

Akim and the others looked at each other with fear in their eyes, and General Rize said, "I understand he's defending himself, but this is overkill, we can't allow him to violate these soldiers like this."

Apollo stopped General Rize from approaching

Seth as he continued to slaughter the other soldiers, Apollo said, "We can't stop him-"

As General Rize responded, "and we also can't allow him to continue."

He shoved Apollo out of the way and rushed toward Seth. He grabbed him by the shoulder and said, "That's enou..." right before he could finish his sentence, Seth backhanded General Rize, knocking him to the ground.

"Stay, out of my way."

Seth started to run his hands through his hair. He struggled to focus on his thoughts, and only heard the woman's voice, "Kill them all. None of them deserve to live, they almost killed your friends."

One of the soldiers saw Seth distracted and shot him in the back, which caused Seth's' pupils to dilate as he turned around and looked at the soldier as if he were prey. As black blood dripped out of his wound all he heard was, "Slaughter them all." Seth, unaffected by the bullets, rushed at the soldier taking him to the ground as he brutally punched his face into the pavement, until his knuckles bled from the concrete. The only thing the group heard was the unpleasant sound of the soldier as he screamed for help, before the scream turned into the sound of his skull being shattered and brains being mushed by Seth's bare fist. Seth finally regained focus and looked at his hands covered in blood, as he sat over his last victim whose head was completely mangled and smeared into the ground. *Did I just black out? No, you're doing exactly what you wanted.* Seth saw the last soldier struggle to walk back to the city. He got a bad headache and struggled to fight his urges. The group approached Seth after they saw that he was clearly in some type of pain.

Akim grabbed Seth's shoulder and said, "Man, we gotta go, and catch up with the others, they're probably waiting on us."

Seth's vision was blurry when he tried to look at Akim. He yelled at Akim with anger in his voice, "GET THE FUCK AWAY FROM ME!"

Then he looked at General Rize and the rest of the group and saw they were on guard. Seth lowered his tone and spoke with this eerie yet unsettling vibe. "Just go on without me, I will catch up."

Seth's heart started to race, and his head throbbed harder. He tried his best to clear his mind, but the only thing he could think about was ripping that last soldier to shreds. Seth screamed in pain. Akim backed away from Seth and the rest followed to the car leaving Seth as he asked. Once they got in the military vehicle, General Rize asked, "Why didn't any of you try to stop him?"

Everyone looked away as Apollo responded, "Seth was the strongest one when we all met for the first time, now that his *blight* has been activated who knows what he is capable of."

Apollo looked at his reflection in the window. His regular eyes stared back at him in that reflection. He continued, "Besides, I don't think any of us are even able to challenge him head - to- head."

Akira added on, "I don't think he wants to hurt anyone anyways, if he did, we wouldn't be alive right now. I think he's struggling. Like Apollo said he's the strongest one, he will find us. He just needs his space."

Everyone was silent as they drove away and watched as Seth followed the soldier who crawled on the ground.

As the group drove away Seth continued to walk toward the last soldier, who left a trail of blood as he struggled to get away. "Man, please, I was just taking orders, please"

Seth closed the gap now and hovered over the soldier. He pressed his foot lightly over the soldiers' neck and asked. "Tell me what the military has planned, and maybe I'll let you live."

The soldier held on to Seth's leg and responded

quickly, "They only commanded us to capture some of you, before you guys get out of Texas."

Seth's thick black blood moved down his arm and into his hand. It slowly manifested into a sword as the soldier continued to speak in fear, "They won't stop coming after you until most of you are dead-"

Seth shoved his sword right through the soldier's mouth, nailing him into the ground. In the last moments of that soldier's life, he struggled to breathe, and he only saw the silhouette of Seth as he looked into his terrifying yet calming purple nebula eyes. Seth watched as the soldier's body twitched.

"If they wish death upon my friends, I will continue to wipe the US Military from the face of the Earth, and anyone else who stands in my way."

Seth stated calmly to corpses he was surrounded by.

Chapter XII

BLIGHT III EVOLUTION

Diana and the rest of the girls just passed Washburn, Texas. They were trying their best to get away from the military base, and they hadn't heard any word from the guys. Diana saw that the truck was running low on gas and stated,

"We are running low on fuel, but we can't stop moving. I don't think we are far enough yet."

Tomie asked, "Does this need gas or diesel? We can't afford to go on foot."

While Ena was looking at a map, Diana responded quickly with a bit of anger and confusion in her voice, "I don't fucking know, we just need to find another means of transportation. I knew we shouldn't have trusted them, now we are separated, and we lost our weapons, and supplies."

Isis tapped her shoulder and replied with a soft tone, "Relax, I'm pretty sure after today Seth won't allow anything like this to happen again. From now on we will do what's best for the group. But we need to stay calm and figure out how to regroup."

Diana took a deep breath, before speaking to Ena, "We passed Washburn, a bit ago. What's coming up next?"

Ena used her finger to guide herself through the map and responded, "Goodnight, Texas. Doesn't seem like much of a city."

Diana nodded and replied, "We will keep going then."

Isis used the radio to try and contact the guys, "Seth, General Rize, anyone there?"

General Rize picked up the radio and responded, "Hey, can you hear me, where are you guys?"

Isis and the rest of the group were pleased to hear a response and replied, "We are close to Goodnight Texas, and running low on fuel. where can we meet up?"

General Rize pointed at a map and Akim who sat in the passenger seat grabbed it and looked around for a moment. He showed General Rize that they just passed Panhandle, Texas, and were also going north away from the others. Throughout this whole conversation, they didn't know that the council of Generals had walkie talkies lined up on different channels eavesdropping.

General Rize gave them instructions, "These vehicles can only run on gas, or diesel, so refuel and make your way to Mclean, Texas. We will regroup there, and get out of Texas, just don't stop moving forward."

Seth was using one of the vehicles from the wreck and forgot about which channel to turn to for the walkie talkie. So, as he drove, he looked around the passenger side, and saw a map. With nothing ahead of him he took brief moments to look at the map. He thought to himself, *Where would they be at, my best option is to get to the border of Texas and meet them there.*

Shortly after he put the map down, he heard someone on the walkie talkie, "They are on their way to Mclean, They aren't planning to stop. We need all soldiers that are available on this task. This group of people could be the ones responsible for the *Collapse.* THEY ARE A HIGH THREAT LEVEL PROCEED WITH CAUTION! We only need one male and one female alive, kill the rest, and collect the corpse."

Seth took off full speed ahead to reunite with the group. One of the generals on the walkies responded, "The helicopters will be prepped for tomorrow, if you can't capture them, do your best to slow them down as much as possible, We cannot allow them to leave Texas."

With the sun setting the girls were now in Groom, Texas with a full tank, unaware of the military plans.

Diana used the walkie talkie to inform the others, "Guys we gotta take it down soon, we are all a bit tired, can you guys make it to Groom, Texas tonight?

General Rize looked around at the others who were either asleep or too tired to care, he responded, "No we might have to take it down too. We can leave first thing in the morning." Seth was in White Deer, Texas stopping for a brief moment to take a piss.

Once he walked off away from the vehicle, the walkie talkie went off, "The girls are in Groom, Texas, and they all seem tired. The men didn't give out any location."

A group responded, "I have a few men, we can be there in ten minutes."

One of the soldiers responded, "Remember, be cautious, and if you can capture the weakest one, kill the rest. Seth came back to the vehicle a few moments later and sat down to take a breather. He heard what seemed to be trucks in the distance, and hid inside the vehicle, peering through the window. He saw two military trucks filled with soldiers slowly cruising by and checking nearby buildings. Once they were out of sight, Seth started driving South to find somewhere to relax.

With the moon taking the sky Diana kept watch while the others were sound asleep, she kept nodding off, not realizing a few vehicles were pulling up in the distance. She shook her head and stood up, walking outside of the building they were camping out for the night. She stretched and paced back and forth to keep herself awake; but in the distance the silence turned into the sound of trucks.

She ran back inside, to wake the others whispering with some volume, "ISIS, TOMIE, ENA get up!!"

They slowly woke up rubbing their eyes, barely making out what Diana said, all were exhausted from the long trip, with barely any food, or water, and no time to sleep. Diana said, "We gotta go before they find us."

A Soldier called out, "It's one of our vehicles here, surround this building."

The soldier used hand signs to position his team, three breaking off in both directions while three stood behind their vehicles pointing their ARs at the entrance. Diana looked at Isis, and her sclera was swallowed by the darkness of her *blight* activating.

"Stay here."

Diana looked out the window and saw past the

lights that there were three people behind the vehicle pointing guns, *They've already surrounded us, I gotta make this fast.* Diana looked at the wall on the side of the building and ran full speed through it, which sent one of the soldiers rolling on the ground. She turned to her left to see two soldiers who were shocked at her bursting through a wall. She grinned, grabbed the closest soldier by the neck, and forced him to the floor, breaking his neck. She tackled the last one who shot her in her stomach as she bit into his throat which made him cough up blood. The other soldiers started running from the other side of the building. Diana grabbed her stomach and saw her black blood drip from her body, she looked up and jumped to the top of the one-story building. She watched as the soldiers blindly ran around the corner, to see their comrades dead on the ground. They saw the one that was sent across the ground, the other with his throat ripped out, and the last one whose neck was snapped. Diana just watched from the rooftop; she used the night to her advantage to hide.

One of the soldiers said, "What the hell could have done this."

The second soldier responded with utter fear in his voice, "There is no way we can capture these animals."

Diana's blood dripped down onto one of the

soldiers. He rubbed it off and looked at his hand, "What the hell is this black stuff?"

The soldier looked up to see a figure in the shadows, with these terrifying yet beautiful eyes. Diana dove at one of the soldiers and caved his chest in with her knee. She turned and tackled the second soldier and used his body as a shield, protecting her from the third soldier who shot at her out of terror. After he ran out of ammo, she threw the corpse at the last soldier which made him fall, and as he struggled to get up she stomped his head multiple times until it was completely mangled. The last three soldiers ran to the side of the building to see Diana standing over their dead comrades.

The leader screamed, "FIRE!" She ducked into the hole she put into the wall.

Diana asked Tomie, "How did you manifest that weapon last time?"

Tomie replied, "When I saw Seth do it, I just thought about how much I wanted to help. I wasn't thinking about anything specific."

Tomie saw the blood coming from Diana's stomach and grabbed her at risk. "Think about how much you want it. Just think about it. Nothing specific. Just a tool, focus on the palm of your hand and the beating of your heart and just manifest it! LET'S DO THIS!" They both nodded at each other as Tomie ran out of the front door flanking them. Diana started to run back to the hole she created while she counted her heartbeat. *One two three, one two three, one two three...come on form now!* When she came back outside a black double-headed spear formed in her hand. Tomie yelled, "Hey right here!" the soldiers turned around, as Diana made the double-headed spear spin, decapitating one of the soldiers. *sheesh she thought, this weapon is something else, I didn't even feel his body.* She followed up by cutting the second soldier in half as she stabbed the third one in the back.

While Diana was holding him with her spear, Tomie walked up to him and asked, "Are there anymore soldiers after us?"

The soldier clenched his teeth, and Tomie asked more forcefully, "Where are the rest of you..." the soldier spit blood in her face and replied, "I'm not telling you anything bitch!"

Ena and Isis walked out to see Tomie grab the last soldier off Diana's spear and force him to the ground. Then she stood on the back of his right shoulder blade and ripped his arm off with brute strength. As he screamed in pain she tossed his arms to the side and kicked him in his face. Tomie wiped the blood off her face and walked away, leaving him there to suffer.

They regrouped and talked for a moment, Tomie said, "There's no way they just found us, do you think that vehicle has a tracker or something?"

Ena shook her head and responded, "no that can't be."

Just then they heard people scream from one of the walkie talkies that was attached to one of the corpses, "ONE OF THEM IS HERE, HE IS WIPING OUT THE WHOLE SQUAD!"

Gunshots could be heard in the background, "He can't be human, he killed twenty of my men please send…"

It cut out and they all looked at each other. Isis said, "That had to be Seth. He's one of the only ones that could wipe out a squad by himself."

They sat in silence for a moment and Ena responded, "twenty men though, what the hell is going on over there."

Tomie added, "As long as he survives that's the only thing that matters, if these people see us as threats so be it."

They walked over to the vehicles the soldiers rode in and grabbed the walkie talkies, Diana realized that one of them was on channel nine and told the others, "They were eavesdropping. That's why they came straight here, we gotta warn the others."

They nodded as Diana used the walkie talkie

and said, "Don't call out any more locations, or give out any information. They are listening."

Ena said, "We can leave the vehicles here, and find somewhere else to rest for the night, and take off first thing in the morning. They all agreed.

General Rize received the message before waking up one of the others to rotate on watch shift. *Damn he thought, now we can't communicate, but the plans don't change, we will all make it out of Texas. I'll let the blight users sleep for now, we will need their strength.* General Rize walked over to Apollo and had him take the watch shift for the night.

Seth found an abandoned farmhouse that he decided to rest in. He couldn't sleep so he went to lay in the grass outside; but every time he tried to sleep; he broke out in a cold sweat. He felt something that he couldn't put his finger on, it felt like a puzzled memory he couldn't piece together, so he just laid there and stared at the stars. He thought to himself, *I gotta' make it back to them. I can't let any of them die. As the strongest I can't allow them to die...* He stayed there in his thoughts until he passed out from exhaustion.

General Rize and the others woke up, they had finally gotten a good sleep, but were still low on food and water. General Rize informed the others that the military was eavesdropping on them, and they now had to make it to McLean, Texas without any communication. They prepared to leave and got into the military vehicle. Akim took the walkie talkie and changed it back to the main channel.

"I don't know why we didn't think of it earlier, but let's see what they are up to. Now we will know where they are coming from." They wasted no time leaving the area, with the sun burning bright in the sky it made the escape more complicated.

Diana and the others finally woke up. They barely had any sleep, and Diana was still fatigued from using her *blight*. Starved, thirsty and deprived of their sleep they had no choice but to move forward as planned.

They walked over to the vehicles and Ena said, "We have a bunch of walkie talkies, and since we can't communicate with the others let's change these extra walkies to different channels to see what else is going on."

Shortly after changing the channels, they heard one of the soldiers through the walkie talkies give a report with total despair in his voice. "We made it to one of the squads we lost connection with... They slaughtered them, at least twenty men completely mutilated, I can't even make out what they did to them. Me and my squad will be leaving panhandle soon, we will keep tracking them."

They all looked at each other, and sat in silence before Diana said, "It sounds like none of us had it easy. That must've been Seth and the others from what we heard yesterday. Let's keep going before they catch up to us." As much as they wanted to just give up, they all knew they couldn't allow the military to get their hands on the *blight*. They proceeded to the vehicles and took off to McLean, Texas.

"Wake up" Seth heard a whisper in his ear, which made him suddenly jolt out of his sleep.

He looked around and saw nothing in sight. Starved, and thirsty he looked off into the distance to see nothing but windmills and open roads, he walked back to the vehicle. He took off to try and catch up with the group; after gaining some distance he heard one of the soldiers on the walkie talkie speak with anger, "We are passing Groom, we have at least ten casualties here, If you encounter these animals, SLAUGHTER THEM!" Seth, saw that Groom was the next city, he stepped on the gas to try and catch up.

Each group heard one of the generals through their walkie talkies. "The helicopters will be taking off soon, all current teams focus on Mclean and don't let them get out of the state.

At this point capture who you can and kill the rest."

They heard multiple squads report back in, and they sat in silence because they knew they needed to kill more people. Not because they wanted to, rather this was simply for survival. Why couldn't the military just help them when they all had the same goal? Without trust, how far can humanity go? Tomie and the others were only halfway to Alanreed, Texas but stopped to recollect themselves.

Tomie walked over to Diana and said, "I'll drive the rest of the way so you could have some time to rest."

Diana nodded, "we can't stop for too long", Ena and Isis just looked off into the distance, in false hope that they were near the end of Texas.

Right before they were getting ready to keep driving, they heard a soldier through the walkie talkie, "I see one of our vehicles in the distance, we are about to encounter them. It looks like four of them are all female. We are halfway past Groom, anyone that is near please hurry."

They all looked at each other and looked behind them to see two military vehicles approaching. They rushed into the vehicle, as one of the soldiers stuck his head out the window and started shooting his AR forcing them to duck. Before Tomie got to drive off, they shot the back tires out, which made her stop. One of the soldiers rammed into them at full speed and forced them to tumble in the car. The five soldiers ran out of the first vehicle, one pointed his gun at them and screamed, "Stay down!" while the other four dragged them out of the car "Get out the fucking truck!"

Tomie tried to fight back "Get off of me!"

Tomie yelled as she bit the soldier's arm and kicked him away. This made him shoot her in the back and caused her to fall to the ground. As she bled, she struggled to activate her *blight*.

Diana yelled, "Get away from her."

She used the back of her head to headbutt the soldier that held her, which broke his nose. The other five soldiers got out of their vehicle, and three of them started to gang up on Diana as they kicked, punched, and stomped on her. She curled up to protect her head.

"Stay down, you piece of shit."

"We are going to fucking kill you."

Ena tried to fight back but she was starved, deprived of sleep and her willpower was unsuccessful in even awakening her *blight*. She struggled to fight two of the soldiers. She swung at one of them, and tried to evade the other, who easily overpowered her. Two soldiers then kicked her in the stomach and head until she stopped resisting.

Isis struggled to get out of the grip of one soldier, and helplessly watched her friends get beaten. S

he cried out, "Stop it, we just wanted to help."

The lead soldier replied and gave out orders, "Shut up! Were you trying to help the men that you slaughtered back there? Separate them, get these two who are dying, get the other two to the truck!"

The soldiers separated Tomie and Diana in the middle of the road. They forced Diana and Tomie to their knees and tied their hands behind their backs, as the lead soldier squatted in front of them. Diana has this odd but familiar feeling that she'd been here before and thought, *If I'm not mistaken this is the end for me, this feels and looks so familiar... almost as if I've been here already.*

The lead soldier said, "I could see it in your eyes, you two pieces of shit are responsible for the death of my squad, and brother..." Tomie interrupted, "You idiots tried to kill us first, we just wanted to help."

He then punched Tomie in the face, and shouted, "Shut up!"

The soldier behind her helped her back up; Diana mumbled, "And look where that got us."

The lead soldier stood in front of Diana and said, "Repeat yourself again."

Diana looked up and said, in a strong Russian accent, "I said, and look where that got us, and look at where it got your sad excuse of a brother. Which one was he?"

Diana laughed while she mocked him, "Was he the one I choked to death, maybe the one that got his throat ripped out? There was also..."

Before she could finish her sentence, the soldier kicked her in her face and yelled, "Shut up!" The other soldiers stopped as the lead soldier pulled out his pistol.

"WE DON'T NEED ALL FOUR OF YOU!"

Diana looked at Isis for the last time, mouthing the words, "I love you; I know you can survive this world without me." As Diana closed her eyes Isis had a rush of memories going through her head. From good memories with her parents, and past life, to the moments where Diana held her and protected her.

While these mixed memories ran through her mind, everything was moving in slow motion for her as she mumbled, "Make it stop, I've had enough. Stop..., stop..., stop, stop..., stop..., stop... stop..." *I love you too.* With a blend of wrath, hate, sadness, regret, and pain in her voice she screamed, "STOOOOOP!" with only Diana in her sight she glared in anger, as her sclera were swallowed in complete darkness, and her iris finally gained that nebula glow. Simultaneously the lead soldier shot while being distracted by Isis; and every living thing that didn't have *blight* energy, life's force was siphoned by Isis. Tomie and Ena struggled to watch. As the soldier slowly shriveled up until it was nothing but burnt skin to bone, no flesh, no muscle. Having no bruises, scratches, or any signs of injury, she ran towards Tomie who was still bleeding out panted in pain and Diana who was shot in the shoulder. Isis embraced both of them in a hug and cried.

Diana chuckled and said, "You gotta' relax, you're too strong to be hugging us that hard."

While Tomie started breath normally and both of their wounds started to heal. Suddenly they didn't feel hungry or thirsty anymore. Isis broke the bondages from Diana and Tomie, then made her way over to Ena who could barely crawl.

Isis knelt and held Ena in her lap as she said, "It's alright, I got you."

Ena's blurry vision became clear as she saw Isis holding her, Ena stared into Isis calming nebula spacey eyes. "You did it, you awakened your *blight*."

Chapter XIII

IT'S NOT YOUR FAULT

As Seth neared a bunch of military vehicles that were stopped in the middle of the road, he slowed down. He looked around and realized a radius of grass seemed to be drained of life. It resembled the colors of ashes. He got out of the vehicle with caution, and slowly walked past the vehicles that blocked the way. He saw charred corpses of some of the military men that surrounded Tomie and Diana who were sitting on the ground. Isis stroked Ena's hair as she rested her head on her lap.

Seth asked with concern in his voice, "What happened here?" The girls were surprised to see him, Diana was the first to get up and respond, "Isis just saved us, she just awakened her *blight* killing all the soldiers around us."

Tomie looked at her stomach and arms, "She even healed us."

Seth walked over to Isis and kneeled in front of her, he softly grabbed her chin so he could look into her eyes.

Seeing the darkness in her sclera and the bright purple in her iris, "You actually did it, and you can heal people."

Seth looked at Ena and asked, "How are you feeling?"

Ena smiled and responded, "Thanks to Isis, I feel great."

Seth smiled and nodded, "That's good." Tomie looked at Seth with concern, she saw the injuries that didn't heal completely, and the blood that covered his clothes.

Tomie asked, "Where are the others?"

Seth lowered his eyes and responded, "I don't know, I told them to go ahead without me, I was slipping out of control from overextending myself, and couldn't remember what channel to contact any of you on. I had to kill a few soldiers and find somewhere to rest before I kept moving forward."

Tomie replied, "If we wait here for a bit, they shouldn't be far off. As far as communication goes, they were eavesdropping on us, this is the second encounter we had with them. So, we changed back to the original channel to keep us a step ahead."

Isis, sclera faded back to white, with a weak voice she said, "Guys we should take a break here, and wait for the others. If Seth made it, that means they can't be too far away. Besides, I think I over did it, I need to rest."

Diana walked over to Isis and helped her into one of the vehicles so she could get out of the sun, "You did good, you really did save us all."

Diana walked back over to the others and said, "She must be fatigued from activating her *blight*. This is perfect while she rests. We'll wait for them to make their way to us. Once we regroup, we gotta' get out of this state."

They agreed, and while they waited, they sat near the trucks using them for shade from the harsh sunlight.

Tomie looked over at Seth and asked, "We heard what happened on the radio... None of us expected we would have to kill to survive. I know everything you do is to protect yourself and us, but how much more do you think you can endure until you're numb to it all? The blood, the bodies, the fear in their eyes. How do you sleep at night?"

Seth looked over at Tomie, understanding that question wasn't really meant for him. He realized she needed some form of comfort and reassurance, he replied, "The whole time we've been fighting, and killing to protect ourselves, and even others; we aren't doing this for fun, and even though we didn't expect for the journey to be this bad, we knew it was going to be dangerous from the start. You gotta' remind yourself... we are in a world with no rules, or government. We are the only ones that have a chance at saving the world."

Seth moved her hair to the side and placed his hand on her cheek. "It's not your fault or any of ours for that matter we are fighting to survive."

Tomie started tearing up, and she embraced Seth, because she didn't want to be seen as she cried.

Moments later a soldier screamed through the walkie talkie, "OUR FIRST TEAM JUST GOT WIPED OUT, IT'S ONLY ONE OF THEM BUT HE CAN'T BE HUMAN! SEND ANOTHER FLEET, SEND THE CHOPPERS, SEND MORE HELP!"

The walkie talkie cut out, and the group grew impatient knowing that they didn't have much time left. Seth and the others huddled around Isis as he explained, "It sounds like they're in trouble. If they don't come within the next ten minutes, Imma' need you all to get out of this state while I retrieve the others.

Diana replied, "We just reunited, we can't be separated again. Even if it's close we will have to wait for them. We can't afford to be divided again."

The other girls agreed which left Seth with no choice but to agree to wait for the others. Right as they finished their conversation another military vehicle approached, which caused Seth to be on guard, until he saw General Rize, and the others get out of the vehicle. As Seth walked to General Rize, the others hugged, just happy to be reunited.

Seth asked, "How much time do you think we have before they catch up to us?"

General Rize responded with no hope in his voice, "We will have to fight sooner or later, we just gotta' get as far as we can for now. I think once we pass the border they will stop tracing us."

He looked off into the distance and continued, "I don't know what happened in Oklahoma, but it can't be as bad as being hunted by the military."

With General Rize calling the shots, they took two of the military trucks to make their final push out of Texas.

As much as they wanted to stop and get some supplies, they had to endure hunger and thirst. In no time they passed Alan reed, and McLean Texas and now they neared Shamrock.

The sun was setting as they heard a soldier on the radio, "We have them in sight, they are approximately twenty miles away from getting out of Texas."

The passengers looked around, "Behind us? No one's around us." and Akira looked up to see a fleet of five helicopters."

The soldiers continued, "Do we have the authorization to attack?"

One of the Generals responded with haste in his voice, "ELIMINATE ALL OF THEM, WE CAN'T ALLOW THEM TO GET OUT OF TEXAS, OKLAHOMA IS A DESIGNATED NO MAN'S LAND. THIS IS OUR LAST STAND. STOP THEM HERE AND NOW WITH ALL THE MIGHT OF THE US MILITARY."

Another General responded on top of that calmly saying, "if we can't stop them here, may God be on our side for what's to come."

General Rize looked at Akira, Akim, Apollo, and Ena with a concerned look on his face and said, "I don't know what you all are capable of, but whatever you have in you, you need to bring it out. Dig deep, find whatever it is inside of you, the will to live, the will to save the world, the will to keep moving forward."

They all nodded, the only one in low spirits was Apollo, *Can I finally do this, if anytime is the right time to awaken the blight it's now. But am I capable of being as strong as Seth.* Ena thought about her father who was strict when it came to the art of war. *Kill or be killed he would say to me. If I keep holding back, I won't make it to New Jersey. I won't be able to make it back to my family. My father will consider me a failure, due to my lack of wanting to be what and who I really am.* They heard the helicopters which were closer. They started firing shots at them.

"We are engaging now."

They tried to drive in an odd pattern, but after a few seconds they hit the engine of General Rize's vehicle making it come to a rough stop.

Seth looked in his rear-view mirror, and said, "It's now or never we gotta' fight them here or they will kill us off!"

Seth stopped and rushed out of the vehicle, while Isis, Diana, and Tomie followed. As they ran back towards the others, General Rize and the others also ran towards them. Seth Looked up as the helicopter started firing again. He looked over at Akim, with both of their sclera faded into darkness and nebula colored iris luminated purple. Seth nodded as he ran directly at Akim who looked back at the helicopters and looked at Seth and nodded back. He kneeled and cuffed his hands together.

Seth used Akim's hands as a platform yelling, "LET'S DO THIS NOW."

Akim used all his might and launched Seth directly at one of the helicopters. Seth grabbed on to the landing skids of one of the helicopters.

One of the soldiers called out, "One of them just jumped onto the helicopter, what the hell are they?"

As Seth proceeded to lift himself up using his upper body strength. The soldier manning the machine gun stepped back as Seth shoved him out of the helicopter. Seth used the machine gun and took out one of the other helicopters that couldn't invade in time.

"We are going down, brace yourselves!"

Tomie and Diana looked at each other as they proceeded to activate their *blight* and follow Akim and Seth's lead.

Diana kneeled, as Tomie stepped back a few yards, "Alright let's go!"

Diana braced her hands together to give Tomie a boost, Tomie ran and put all her weight into her feet, as Diana launched her as far as possible.

One of the soldiers called it out, "Another one is airborne can they fucking fly?"

As Tomie landed on the front windshield she thought, *Seth is fucking insane.* She punched through the window grabbed the pilot out by his collar and held him as the helicopter spun out of control. With two helicopters being out of the way Seth took the pistol from the pilot's holster and shot him which forced the helicopter to crash into the one next to him. With only one helicopter left it retreated as Tomie braced herself using the soldier as cushion while the helicopter crashed. Seth walked out of the crash, cut up and bleeding. As they regrouped,

Seth tried to control his urges, "We gotta' keep going, we should be halfway there."

They all followed his lead and ran towards Oklahoma as it was only a few miles away at this point. They fluctuated between running and jogging. Once the night started to settle in, they could hear a herd of trucks in the distance, alongside were two more helicopters. They all looked back, in disbelief.

Seth slowed down, and stated his plan, "Apollo, Ena, Rize, and Isis stay back, I will lead the assault. Just stay behind me." Seth ran toward the herd of trucks, breathing heavily.

He thought, *It's my responsibility as the strongest to lead them to safety and I won't allow anyone to harm them!* Seth manifested his sword as the helicopter started shooting at him. He noticed some of the trucks drove past him. As he dodged the bullets he looked back at the trucks and thought *they must be trying to cut off the exit and send more soldiers.* Akim and Akira, activated their *blight* and ran directly at the trucks that passed Seth. Akim jumped into the window of one of the vehicles, and strangled the driver which forced them to crash. Akira jumped on the front hood of one of the other vehicles. He broke through the window and pulled out the driver tossing him outside. Akira then proceeded to turn the wheel and forced the vehicle to veer to the right. As it flipped, he jumped off, and landed effortlessly. Diana and Tomie started to run back to help Seth. They knew they couldn't let him fight alone. Ena followed behind them and thought to herself, *I've been holding back my whole life, and now is the time to let go of my childish acts. We all need each other more than ever, it's time to embrace what I was made to be. A Leader. A Fighter.* Ena's eyes were engulfed by darkness, as her Iris' finally glowed like the stars in the universe. There were six trucks they set up in front of Seth like a blockade. Before the soldiers could fire, Seth used one of the vehicles to jump into one of the helicopters. Seth pounced on the soldier who was manning the machine gun. He punched him in his chest until his ribcage was crushed. From a distance, Isis looked at her hands and then at the other helicopter, *Just like Tomie explained, I need to just focus*! Isis' eyes were swallowed by darkness as she used her right hand as a grip and left hand as if she was pulling back an arrow. When she pulled harder and her heartbeat increased, fragments of a black bow manifested, from the grip to the string, followed by an arrow. Diana, Tomie, and Ena, started off their assault by dodging bullets, and ducking behind the vehicles.

Diana said, "There's at least twenty of them, are

you ready?"

Tomie, breathed heavily and responded, "Ready as I'll ever be."

As Ena nodded, "I'm done holding back."

They both saw that Ena awakened her *blight*, as Isis held something in the distance. The moment the bow was done manifesting, Isis smirked knowing that the billions of dollars that the United States used to buy their equipment, was nothing compared to what the *blight* was capable of. She shot at the helicopter, with the arrow piercing through the pilot and helicopter as if it were paper. As the helicopter fell and crashed into some of the soldiers, Apollo and General Rize watched in awe, and knew interfering would be a liability to the rest of them. Apollo thought to himself, *Even Isis could activate her blight, and I can't even imagine the idea of me doing so. Am I really just that weak?* While Tomie and Ena were stunned for a moment, Ena capitalized off Isis' attack, as she hopped over the vehicle, and jumped on the back of one of the distracted soldiers. She snapped his neck and took his AR. Then she shot all the others that stood in front of her. As the soldiers behind her tried to shoot her, Diana jumped in the way taking a few bullets to the stomach, as Tomie followed up and grabbed the soldier from behind. She put him in a chokehold and snapped his neck. After Seth saw the other helicopter was down, he instructed the pilot to land.

The pilot screamed, "If I die, you're all coming with me, you animals!"

The pilot tried to dive directly at Tomie, Diana and Ena. Seth redirected the helicopter and saved them, but he crashed with the pilot. They all rushed over after the fight was over, and saw Seth rise from the crash, holding his arm, and breathing heavily. They realized he was no longer healing properly, with gashes and cuts on his arms and face, bleeding out.

He said, "We did it, now we just have a few more miles until Oklahoma."

Akim walked over to help Seth to one of the trucks, "Let's go."

They took two of the vehicles, and with the short drive they made their way to Oklahoma. The entrance of Texola seemed like a ghost town. They got out of the vehicles to look for somewhere to bunker for the night. They were exhausted, hungry, and sleep deprived. Finally done running from the military, all they could think about was what would come next. Why was the military so afraid to enter Oklahoma? Seth had a bad feeling in his gut and right when he looked over at the group, something that ran at full speed tackled Apollo and they both slid on the ground. Everyone stood there as something hovered over Apollo. Seth and the others struggled to activate their *blight* since they were heavily fatigued.

The thing responded as the moonlight shone on its face and it said in a raspy voice, "I found you guys."

Under the moonlight they saw this person's nails and teeth as sharp as knives, as if he was some type of animal, his clothes were drenched in blood, and his voice sounded oddly familiar.

But the thing that shook them to their core, were his eyes, he had the *blight*. His sclera was black, and his iris was a dim purple.

As Apollo tried to crawl away, Seth asked, "What are you?"

The question seemed to irritate the thing, as it started to mumble, "After everything you really don't remember me? YOU ALL THOUGHT I WAS WEAK?!"

The thing started to pace back and forth over Apollo's body.

"I just wanted to be as strong as you all, I just wanted to be capable of protecting my friends, just like you Seth."

The moment he said that Seth put it all together and said softly, "Brian?"

The group grew silent as Seth approached him

and continued, "Look at yourself, what did you do?" Brian looked at the fear in their eyes, and then his hands.

Seth said, "We can help you, just tell us what happened to Colby and Bellatrix."

Brian looked up and everything that Seth said was muffled and replaced with other words brought on by his skewed thoughts, "You will always be weak. That's why we left you behind, that's why all your friends are dead."

Seth tried to place his hands on his shoulder, and Brian scratched him forcing him to fall back. "If you think I'm so weak then stop me, IF I HAD TO LOSE IT ALL, SO DO YOU!"

Brian proceeded to shove his fist into Apollo's chest, everything went silent for him as everyone else screamed. Seth's vision grew blurry as he rushed at Brian with nothing but rage, and hate. Brian evaded Seth's first attack and rushed General Rize, who couldn't react fast enough. Brian forced him to the ground and gutted him, Isis rushed over to Apollo who had a hole in his chest. While Ena, Tomie and Diana surrounded Brian. They looked over at Apollo who was laid out on the ground, and now their new enemy Brian smirked and rushed at Ena who countered his grappling, throwing him into the ground. Diana followed up with an axe kick and aimed for his head, he dodged it by rolling which then caused Diana to leave a small crater in the pavement.

Tomie grabbed at his leg and called out, "SETH NOW!"

Seth manifested his sword and attempted to plunge it into Brian aiming for his head. Once the smoke cleared Seth realized he missed, Brian smiled and kicked Seth off him. Isis struggled to heal Apollo and looked over to see General Rize gutted with his stomach, intestines and other organs hanging out of his body. Diana rushed to help Tomie pin Brian to the floor, as Seth got back up and stepped on his chest. Seth then proceeded to shove his sword into Brian's neck which caused him to choke on his blood. He shoved his sword into Brian's chest to finish him off.

As Brian began to weaken because death was imminent for him his sclera faded back to white, and he mumbled, "I just wanted to be as strong as all of you."

The others rushed over to Apollo, while Seth kept stabbing Brian's corpse partly to make sure he was dead, but mostly from all the pent-up rage he felt within himself ... the feeling of being weak ... the feeling of failure ... the feeling of hopelessness. Then he decapitated him. Seth walked over to see Apollo's weak body, as the rest of the group cried on their knees and hovered over him.

Seth moved them out of the way and leaned over Apollo, "COME ON AWAKEN YOUR *BLIGHT*! YOU'RE TELLING ME YOU DON'T WANT TO LIVE?!"

Apollo's vision grew blurry as he thought to himself. *I do want to live. I'm dying because I was too weak. I was never as great as the rest of you. I can't even save myself. How could I ever protect any of you.*

Seth glared at Isis and yelled, "SAVE HIM, YOU CAN HEAL PEOPLE RIGHT! SAVE HIM."

Isis cried and replied, "I can't."

Seth's anger mixed with sadness and hate as he started to cry, "What do you mean you can't save him, NOW!"

Diana grabbed at Seth's shoulder, and she tried to calm him down, "Seth there is nothing we can do."

Seth shrugged his shoulder from her grip, "There has to be a way."

Seth's heart raced as he heard a woman's voice, "So you were too weak to protect just one of your friends, how will you protect the others? They are too weak to survive in this world. You are the only exception... just forget about them."

Tomie said, "Seth there is nothing you can do."

The only thing that echoed in Seth's head was, *Nothing I can do.* Those words pierced his heart and made something in his head snap. Seth grabbed Tomie by the neck with both of his hands and started choking her.

"Nothing that I can do? I SHOULD'VE KILLED BRIAN THE MOMENT, WE SAW HIM!"

The others tried to pull Seth off Tomie as she struggled to gasp for air. Akim had him in a head lock while Diana and Ena were trying to restrain his arms, and Akira grabbed at his waist trying to pull him back. They struggled to pry him off, because his wrath now fueled his power which made him uncontrollable.

He continued, "DON'T TELL ME IT'S NOTHING I WOULDN'T DO, I COULD'VE SAVED HIM!"

Akim tried to strengthen his grip, Seth just head butted him with the back of his head which forced Akim to the ground and his nose to bleed.

Tomie stopped grabbing at his arms and slowly held his face mummering with her last breath, "It's not your fault."

Seth loosened his grip and cried while laying over Tomie, as she hugged him and said it again, "It's not your fault or any of ours."

As everyone else sat in despair and mourned Apollo's death, under the moonlight.

AFTER THE COLLAPSE THERE IS CARNAGE